The Three Strange Travellers

and

Other Stories

by
ENID BLYTON

Illustrated by
Val Biro

AWARD PUBLICATIONS LIMITED

For further information on Enid Blyton please conatct
www.blyton.com

ISBN 1–84135–481–3

This edition entitled *The Three Strange Travellers and Other Stories*
published by permission of Enid Blyton Limited

First Published by Award Publications Limited 2000
This edition first published 2006

Published by Award Publications Limited, The Old Riding
School, Welbeck Estate, Worksop, Notts. S80 3LR

Printed in Singapore

CONTENTS

The Three Strange Travellers

Once upon a time there was a billy-goat who drew a little goat-carriage on the sea-sands. He took children for quite a long ride along the beach.

But one day, when he was quite old, he became lame. He limped with his right front foot, and no longer could he draw the goat-carriage along at a fine pace.

"You are no use to me now," said his master, a cross and selfish old man. "I shall buy a new goat."

The old billy-goat bleated sadly. What would he do if his master no longer needed him?

"You can go loose on the common," said the old man. "Don't come to me for a home, for I don't want you any longer."

Poor billy-goat! He was very unhappy.

He looked at his little goat-carriage for the last time and then he limped off to the common. The winter was coming on and he hoped he would not freeze to death. He had always lived in a cosy shed in the wintertime – but now he would have no home.

He hadn't gone very far across the common when he heard a loud quacking behind him. "Quack quack! Stop, I say! Hey, stop a minute! Quack!"

The billy-goat turned round. He saw a duck waddling along as fast as it could, quacking loudly.

"What's the matter?" he asked.

"Plenty!" said the duck, quite out of breath. "Do you mind if I walk with you? There are people after me who will kill me if they find me."

"Mercy on us!" said the goat, startled. "Why do they want to kill you?"

"Well," said the duck indignantly, "I have stopped laying eggs and my master says I'm no use now, so he wants to eat me for his dinner. And I have served him well for many many months, laying him delicious eggs, far nicer than any hen's!"

"Dear me," said the billy-goat, "you and I seem to have the same kind of masters. Maybe they are brothers. Well, Duck, walk with me. I am seeking my fortune, and would be glad of company."

The two walked on together, the goat limping and the duck waddling. When they reached the end of the common they came to a farm.

"Do not go too near," said the duck. "I don't wish to be caught. Do you?"

"No," said the goat. "Listen! What's that?"

They stood still and heard a great

7

barking. Suddenly a little dog squeezed itself under a near-by gate and came running towards them. The duck got behind the goat in fright, and the goat stood with his horns lowered in case the dog should attack him.

"Don't be afraid of me," panted the dog. "I am running away. My master has beaten me because I let a fox get two chickens last night. But what could I do? I was chained up and I could not get at the fox. I barked loudly, but my master was too fast asleep to hear me. And now he blames me for the fox's theft!"

"You are to be pitied," said the goat. "We, too, have had bad masters. Come with us, and we will keep together and look after ourselves. Maybe we shall find better masters some day."

"I will come," said the dog. "I am getting old, you know, and I cannot see as well as I used to do. I think my master wants to get rid of me and have a younger dog. Ah me, there is no kindness in the world these days!"

The three animals journeyed on

together. They ate what they could find. The billy-goat munched the green grass; the duck swam on each pond she came to and hunted about in the mud at the bottom for food; the dog sometimes found a bit of bread or a hunk of meat thrown away by the wayside, which he gobbled greedily.

They walked for miles and miles. Often the goat and the dog gave the duck a ride on their backs for she waddled so slowly and soon got tired. At night they found a sheltered place beneath a bush, or beside a haystack, and slept there in

a heap, the duck safely in the middle.

They became very fond of one another and vowed they would never separate. But as the days grew colder the three creatures became anxious.

"When the ponds are frozen I shall find no food," said the duck.

"And I shall not be able to eat grass when everywhere is covered with snow," said the goat. "I shall freeze to death at night, too, for I have always been used to a shed in the winter."

"And I have been used to a warm kennel," said the dog. "What shall we do?" They could think of no plan, so on they wandered.

Then one afternoon a great snowstorm blew up. The blizzard was so strong that even the soft snowflakes stung their eyes.

"We shall be completely lost in this dreadful storm!" barked the dog. "We must find shelter."

The goat and the duck followed him. He put his nose to the ground and ran off. He went up a little hill and at last

came to a small cottage. There was a light in one of the windows.

"Somebody lives here," said the dog. "Let us knock at the door and ask for shelter."

So the goat tapped the door with his hoof. He bleated as he did so, and the dog whined and the duck quacked.

Inside the cottage was an old woman with a red shawl round her shoulders. She was darning a hole in a stocking, and thinking about the dreadful storm. Suddenly she heard the tap-tap-tapping at her door.

"Bless us!" she cried, in a fright. "There's someone there! Shall I open the door or not? It may be a robber come through the storm to rob me of the gold pieces I have hidden so carefully in my old stocking under the mattress! No, I dare not open the door!"

As she sat trembling she heard the dog whining. Then she heard the bleating of the goat and the anxious quacking of the duck.

"Well, well!" she said in astonishment.

"It sounds for all the world like a dog, a goat and a duck! But how do they come to my door like this? Do they need shelter from this terrible storm, poor things? Well, I have no shed to put them in, so they must come in here with me."

She got up and went to the door. She undid the bolt and opened the door a crack. When she saw the trembling goat, the shivering dog and the frightened duck her kind heart melted at once and she opened the door wide.

"Poor lost creatures!" she said. "Come in, come in. You shall have warmth and shelter while this storm lasts. Then I've

no doubt you will want to go back to your homes."

The three animals came gladly in to the warmth. The dog at once lay down on the hearth-rug, the goat stood near by, and the duck lay down in a corner, put her head under her wing and fell fast asleep, for she was very tired.

The old woman didn't know what to make of the three creatures. They seemed to know one another so well, and by the way they bleated, barked and quacked to one another they could talk as well as she could.

The goat was very thin, and the dog was skinny, too. As for the duck, when the old woman felt her, she was nothing but feathers and bone!

"The poor creatures," said the kind old dame. "They are starving. Well, I will give them a good meal to eat – they will feel all the better for it."

So she began to cook a meal of all the household scraps she had – bits of meat, vegetables, potatoes, bread, all sorts. How good it smelled! Even the duck in the

corner stuck out her head from under her wing to have a sniff.

The old woman took the big saucepan off the fire and stood it on the windowsill to cool. Then she ladled the warm food out into three dishes and put one in front of each animal.

"There, my dears," she said, "eat that and be happy tonight."

Well, the three animals could hardly

believe their eyes to see such kindness! They gobbled up the food and left not a single scrap. Then the goat rubbed his head gently against the old dame's knee, the dog licked her hand and the duck laid her head on her shoe. Then they all curled up in a heap together and fell asleep. The old dame went to her bed and slept, too.

In the morning the storm was over. The countryside was covered with snow. The animals did not want to leave the warm cottage, but the old woman opened the door.

"Now you must find your way home," she said. She did not know that they had no homes. She thought they had got lost in the storm, and that now they would be glad to go out and find their way back to their homes.

The animals were sad. They took leave of the kind woman, and wished they could tell her that they would like to stay. But she could not understand their language. They went out into the snow, and wondered where to go next.

"Let us go down the hill," said the goat. "See, there are some haystacks there and we may be able to find some food and shelter under the stacks tonight."

So down the hill they went. But they could not find any food. They crouched under the haystack that evening and tried to get warm. As they lay there, quite still, they heard the sound of soft footsteps in the snow. Then they heard voices.

"The old woman has a great hoard of gold," said one voice. "We will go to her cottage tonight, when she is in bed, and steal it."

"Very well," said the second voice. "I will meet you there, and we will share the gold. She has no dog to bark or bite."

The animals listened in horror. Why, it must be the kind old woman these horrid men were speaking of! How

could they save her from the robbers?

"We must go back to the cottage," said the dog. "Somehow we must creep in and wait for these robbers. Then we will set on them and give them the fright of their lives!"

So the three limped, walked and waddled all the way up the hill again until they came to the little cottage. The old woman was just going to bed. The goat peeped in at the window and saw her blow her candle out.

"She has left this window a little bit open," he said to the dog. "Can you jump in and open the door for me and the duck?"

"Yes," said the dog, "I can do that. I often saw my master open the farm doors. I know how to."

He squeezed in through the window and went to the door. He pulled at the latch and the door opened. It was not bolted, so the goat and the duck came in at once. They could hear the old dame snoring.

"What shall we do when the robbers

come?" asked the duck excitedly.

"I have a plan," said the goat. "You, duck, shall first of all frighten the robbers by quacking at the top of your very loud voice. You, dog, shall fly at the legs of the first robber, and I will lower my head and butt the second one right in the middle. Ha, what a fright we will give them!"

The three animals were so excited that they could hardly keep still. The duck flew up on the table and stood there. The dog hid behind the door. The goat stood ready on the hearth-rug, for he wanted a good run when he butted the second robber.

Presently the dog's sharp ears told him that the two robbers were outside. He warned the others and they got ready to do their parts. The robbers pushed the door open.

At that moment the duck opened her beak and quacked as loudly as she could. How she quacked! Quack! Quack! Quack! Quack! Quack!

Then the dog flew at the legs of the

first robber and bit them. And he growled. Grrrr! Grrrr! Wuff! Wuff! Wuff! What a terrible noise it was!

Then the goat ran at the second robber and butted him so hard in the middle that he sat down suddenly and lost all his breath.

The duck was so excited that she

wanted to join in the fun. So she flew at the robbers and pecked their noses hard. Peck! Peck!

The robbers were frightened almost out of their lives. They couldn't think what was happening! There was such a terrible noise going on, and something was biting, hitting and pecking them from top to toe. How they wished they had never come near the cottage!

As soon as they could they got to their feet and ran. The duck flew after them and pecked their ankles. The dog tore pieces out of their trousers. The goat limped as fast as he could and butted them down the hill. My, what a set-to it was!

The two robbers fell into a ditch and covered themselves with mud.

"That old woman is a witch!" cried one.

"Yes, she pinched my ears!" said the other. "And she bit my legs!"

"Ho, and she punched me in the middle so that I lost all my breath!" said the first.

"And all the time she was making such a noise!" cried the second, trying to clamber out of the ditch. "She said: 'Whack! Whack! Whack!'"

"Yes, and she cried: 'Cuff! Cuff! Cuff!' too!" said the first. "And how she chased us down the hill!"

The three animals laughed till the tears came into their eyes when they heard the robbers talking like this.

"They thought my 'Quack, quack, quack!' was 'Whack, whack, whack!'" said the duck, in delight.

"And they thought my 'Wuff, wuff, wuff!' was 'Cuff, cuff, cuff!'" said the dog, jumping about joyfully. "What a joke! How we frightened them!"

23

"Let us go back and see if the old dame is all right," said the goat. "She awoke when the duck began to quack."

Back they all went to the cottage, and found the old dame sitting up in bed, trembling, with a lighted candle by her side. When she saw the three animals she could hardly believe her eyes.

"So it was you who set upon those robbers and chased them away!" she said. "You dear, kind, clever creatures! Why, I thought you had gone to your homes!"

The goat went up to the bed and put his front paws there. The dog put his nose on the quilt. The duck flew up on the bed-rail and flapped her wings.

"Wuff!" said the dog, meaning: "We want to stay with you!"

"Bleat!" said the goat, and meant the same thing.

"Quack!" said the duck, and she meant the same thing too.

And this time the old dame understood them, and she smiled joyfully.

"So you want to stay here?" she said. "Well, you shall. I'm all alone and I want

24

company. It's wintertime and I expect you need shelter, so you shall all live with me. I shall always be grateful to you for chasing away those robbers."

Well, those three animals soon settled down with the old woman. The duck laid her an egg for her breakfast each day. The dog lay on the doormat and guarded the cottage for her each night. The goat was troubled because he could do nothing for his kind mistress.

But one day he found how well he could help her. She had to go to the woods to get firewood. She took with her a little cart to bring it back, and this she had to pull herself, for she had no pony.

But the goat stood himself in the shafts and bleated. The old woman saw that he wanted her to tie the cart to him so that he might pull the wood home for her, and she was delighted. Every day after that the goat took the cart to the woods

for his mistress and very happy they were together.

As for the robbers, they have never dared to come back. They went a hundred miles away, and told the people there a marvellous story of an old witch who cried "Whack! Cuff! Whack! Cuff!" and could bite, pinch and punch all at once. But nobody believed them.

The old dame and the dog, goat and duck still live together very happily. Their house is called Windy Cottage, so if ever you pass by, go in and see them all. The old dame will love to tell you the story of how they came to live together!

The Marvellous
Pink Vase

Once upon a time Mr and Mrs Squabble went to a fair. Mr Squabble spent sixpence on hoopla, and tried to throw wooden rings over the things spread out on a table. Mrs Squabble spent threepence, and she was very lucky. One of her rings fell right over a marvellous pink vase.

It was very tall, and had pink roses painted all the way up. Mrs Squabble was simply delighted with it. When the man gave it to her she beamed with joy.

"Isn't it lovely?" she said to Mr Squabble as she carried it home. "I wonder where I should put it."

Now Mr Squabble only liked vases when they were put so high up on a shelf or bookcase that he couldn't knock them over. So he made up his mind that he would say the vase would look fine on the top of the grandfather clock.

When they got home Mrs Squabble put the pink vase down on the table and looked round her parlour. "Now where shall I put it?" she said. "It must be some place where every one will see it, because it really is beautiful."

"Well, my dear, I should put it on the top of the grandfather clock," said Mr Squabble at once.

"On the top of the clock!" said Mrs Squabble, in surprise. "What a silly place!

You never put anything on top of grandfather clocks."

"Well, why not?" asked Mr Squabble. "It would be quite a new place. I should love to see it there. Then, whenever I looked to see the time, which I do quite twenty times a day, I should see the vase. It's a marvellous place."

"Well, I don't think so," said Mrs Squabble firmly. "I shall put it on this little table here, near your armchair."

Mr Squabble looked on in horror as he watched Mrs Squabble put the vase on a rickety little table near his chair. He knew quite well that the first time he reached out for his pipe he would knock the vase over.

"Now, my dear," he said, "that's a foolish place. Only a woman would think of such a silly place."

"Oh! How dare you say a thing like that!" cried Mrs Squabble. "Just because I didn't like the top of the grandfather clock!"

"Well, if you don't like that, what about putting the vase safely up there on the

shelf, beside the radio?" said Mr Squabble, trying to speak in a nice peaceful voice.

"Really, Squabble, you do think of some stupid places!" said Mrs Squabble. "Why, every time you turned on the radio the vase might be knocked over."

"I don't think so," said Mr Squabble. "Though if you turned on the radio when that dreadful woman with the screeching voice sings, the vase might jump right off in alarm."

"I'll put the vase on the mantelpiece," said Mrs Squabble. But that didn't suit Mr Squabble at all.

"I shall knock it over when I reach up for the matches," he said.

"Clumsy person!" said Mrs Squabble.

"Indeed I'm not!" said Mr Squabble. "Why, I could walk on flowerpots all round the parlour and not fall off once. And that's more than you could do!"

Well, of course, that was quite enough to make Mrs Squabble fetch in twenty flowerpots from the shed and stand them round the parlour.

"All right!" she said. "Now we'll just see who is clumsy and who is not! You start walking on the flowerpots that side, and I'll start walking on them this side. And whoever falls off first has lost, and the other one can choose where to put the pink vase. And let me tell you this, Squabble – that I shall win without any doubt at all!"

The two of them started to walk on the upturned flowerpots. They did look silly. Round the parlour they went, and round and round, neither of them falling off, for they were being very, very careful.

And then the cat jumped in at the parlour window and made both Mr and Mrs Squabble jump so much that they

fell off their flowerpots at the same moment and fell *crash* against the little table.

The pink vase was there. It wobbled – it fell over – it rolled off the table – it tumbled to the floor with a bang – and it smashed into a hundred pieces!

The cat sat in a corner and washed itself. "Now they'll both know where to put the marvellous pink vase!" the cat purred to itself. "There's only one place now – and that's the dustbin!"

Mr Stamp-About
in a Fix

"I've written three times to Mr Tiles to tell him to come and mend my roof," said Mr Stamp-About to his sister. "And what does he say? He says he's too busy. Pah! Too busy to mend my roof? Just wait till I see him!"

"Please don't stamp on that rug," said his sister. "You're making the dust fly about. I think it's because you're so bad-tempered that people won't come and do things for you. Now stop stamping. If you want to beat the dust out of that rug, take it out, hang it over the line and beat it."

"Pah!" said Mr Stamp-About, and stalked out of the room. He put on his hat and went to find Mr Tiles. He was in his shed, getting ready to go and do a job.

Mr Stamp-About caught hold of him. "Ha! I suppose you were just about to come and mend my roof. Now don't you dare to say you weren't. You come along with me this minute!"

Little Mr Tiles looked at big, fierce Mr Stamp-About. "Let go," he said. "If you force me to go with you like this I'll have to come – but I won't put your tiles on properly, so there!"

"Oh, yes, you will!" said Mr Stamp-About. "Because I'll sit by you and watch you! And not a penny will you get if you don't do your best work. Now bring some tiles along with you, and a pot of paint, too, to touch up the gutters. And I shall sit on a chimney pot and watch you!"

"You will, will you?" said little Mr Tiles. "Right. I'll get the tiles – here they are. And I'll bring this pot and this brush along with me. Off we go!"

And off they went together, Mr Stamp-About holding on fast to Mr Tiles in case he ran off. But he didn't. He walked along quite amiably, and talked about the weather.

"Fetch the ladder," said Mr Stamp-About, when they got to his house. "It's in my shed. Climb up it first and begin to put on the new tiles. I'm going to have a cup of hot cocoa as it's a cold day. Then I'll come up the ladder and sit on a chimney pot to watch you. I'll have a fine view of your work, I can tell you!"

Mr Tiles went to fetch the ladder. He set it up against the gutter and climbed up. Mr Stamp-About had disappeared into the house to get his cocoa. Dear, dear – he hadn't even thought of offering cold Mr Tiles a cup. Still, that suited Mr

Tiles all right. He had something to do before Mr Stamp-About came out again!

He climbed the ladder quickly, taking his tiles with him. He set them down on the roof and then went back for his pot and his brush. He grinned as he brought those up. He took a quick look down. Mr Stamp-About was nowhere to be seen. He was somewhere in the house, having cocoa and biscuits.

Mr Tiles looked at the two chimneys sticking up out of the roof. One was smoking. One wasn't, so that was the one that Mr Stamp-About would sit on to watch Mr Tiles doing his work. Aha!

Mr Tiles climbed up to the chimney pot. It was squat and round. He took his brush and dipped it into his pot. He painted the rim of the pot round and round. But not with paint. Oh, no! There was no paint in that pot – there was nice sticky glue! Aha, Mr Stamp-About, you didn't know that, did you, because the pot was labelled WHITE PAINT!

Mr Tiles grinned. He slid down to where the roof needed new tiles and set to work. Presently he heard Mr Stamp-About climbing up the ladder. He saw him clambering up to the chimney pot

and sitting himself flat down on it, just as if it were a stool. Mr Tiles grinned to himself.

"Now, get on, Tiles," said Stamp-About. "I can see everything you do. You're to work well and quickly. I'm not going to pay you too much, either."

"You're going to pay me twenty pounds," said Mr Tiles. "Or your sister is. Twenty pounds, Mr Stamp-About – part-payment for this work, and part-payment for your bad temper!"

If Mr Stamp-About hadn't been stuck fast to the chimney pot he would have fallen off in rage. He stamped his feet on the roof and loosened another tile.

"That's no good!" said Mr Tiles. "That will cost you even more for another tile. Still, stamp about, Stamp-About. I don't mind you paying me more money!"

Stamp-About shouted and stamped. Mr Tiles took no notice. He finished his work and went down the ladder. "Twenty-one pounds!" he shouted to Stamp-About. "I'll get it from your sister as I'm sure you won't give it to me!"

Mr Stamp-About tried to get up from his chimney-pot seat, but he couldn't. Something seemed to be holding him back. What could it be?

"Come back! Don't you dare to ask my sister to pay you!" he yelled. "I'll pay you ten pounds and that's too much!"

"Goodbye," said Mr Tiles, jumping off the ladder. "Be careful you don't loosen any more tiles!"

He went into the house and told Stamp-About's sister she was to pay him twenty-one pounds. She took it out of the cash-box and gave it to him. He beamed and went out.

"Where's my brother?" called the sister. "I must just make certain the amount is right."

"He won't come in for a bit," said Mr Tiles with a grin. "You can ask him then."

Off he went, looking back now and again to see the furious Mr Stamp-About. There he sat on the chimney, trying his best to get up, but the glue was much too strong for him. He raged and

stamped and shouted, and soon a collection of interested people came to watch.

"I'm stuck, I'm stuck!" he yelled. "Get me down!"

But people were afraid of his bad temper, and, besides, they were pleased to see horrid old Stamp-About stuck up on his own chimney pot. And would you

41

believe it, there he had to stay till a downpour of rain came and thinned out the glue.

Poor Mr Stamp-About. He was soaked through, and he missed his footing as he climbed down the roof, bounced down the ladder, and landed with a bump on the ground.

"Stamp-About! What do you think you are doing, sitting on a chimney pot, shouting and yelling like that, and then falling off the roof?" cried his sister. "I'm ashamed of you. You can go straight up to bed. I've had enough of you today!"

And you'll hardly believe it, but Stamp-About had had such a lesson that he did go straight up to bed. He never forgot his day on the chimney pot – and neither did anyone else!

Goofy Isn't Very Clever

"Now, Goofy, if you lose your handkerchief again I shall be very angry with you," his mother said. "It's only Wednesday – and you've lost four hankies already this week."

"Sorry, Ma," said Goofy.

"It's no good being sorry if you keep on doing the same thing," said his mother. "If you're really sorry you won't lose a single hanky again this week!"

"Ma, I won't," said Goofy earnestly, "I really won't, Ma. If I do you can take all the money out of my money-box to buy new hankies, and you can send me to bed with nothing to eat but bread. There now – surely that will make you believe I'm really sorry and I mean what I say about not losing any more hankies!"

His mother looked at him. "All right, I believe you, Goofy," she said. "But that's a dreadful lot of punishments you're laying up for yourself! You'd better be very careful. Look at your hanky now!"

Goofy looked. It was hanging half out of his pocket, just ready to drop. He stuffed it back, but changed his mind and pulled it right out.

"I'm going to pin it on me, Ma," he said. "Then I can't possibly lose it."

"Well, here's my very biggest safety-pin," said his mother, and she gave Goofy an enormous one. "Now let me see you pin your hanky on your front."

Goofy solemnly pinned it there. He

smacked himself on the chest.

"Now I'm safe! The hanky can't possibly be lost, so don't you worry any more, Ma!" He went off to get the basket to do the shopping.

His mother called after him:

"Goofy! Don't you forget to put your sunhat on, now – the sun is blazing down today, and you'll get sunstroke again if you go without your hat."

"Right, Ma!" called Goofy, and went to the cupboard for the shopping basket. He came out with it, and carefully put the shopping-list in the bottom of the basket. Oh, Goofy was going to be very, very careful about everything now! He'd show his mother he could be trusted.

He went off down the street. He quite forgot to fetch his sunhat before he started out! The sun blazed down, tremendously hot. Goofy toiled along, panting.

He met Dame Slow. She called out to him:

"Goofy! What's your mother thinking of to send you out without your sunhat?

45

You'll get sunstroke again as sure as eggs are eggs!"

Goofy put his hand up to his head. His hair was burning hot! Goodness gracious, he'd forgotten his sunhat after all! Now he would get sunstroke and feel sick again, and have a dreadful headache!

"I can't go all the way home again to fetch my hat," groaned Goofy. "What can I do?" Then he thought of a splendid idea. "Of course! I'll knot my big hanky at the corners and wear it like a cap! Then I'll be quite all right."

He unpinned the big safety-pin and took his hanky off his chest. He carefully pinned the safety-pin back again, so as not to lose it. Then he knotted his hanky at the corners, and made a very nice little cap of it.

He slipped it over his hot head. Ah – that was better. Now he'd be all right! He went off happily to the shops, feeling very, very clever.

He did all the shopping quite well. Then he set off home again, thinking how pleased his mother would be with

him. She might even give him a slice of the new fruit cake!

Now, just as he was going in at the front gate he sneezed.

Whooooosh-oo! He felt for his hanky at once – but, dear me, it wasn't on his chest. Goofy stared down at himself in dismay.

"Now I've gone and lost my hanky again!" he groaned. "How could it have gone? The big safety-pin is still there on my chest – but the hanky isn't. It isn't in my pockets, either. Oh, dear, oh, dear, it's gone!"

His mother was out. Goofy felt very, very sad. He remembered the punishment he had told his mother she could give him if he lost his hanky again.

He put the shopping on the table. He went to the larder and cut himself two slices of dry bread. He took his money-box and emptied it out on the kitchen table and wrote a little note beside it: *To buy a new hanky.*

Then he climbed slowly upstairs, undressed himself and put himself to bed.

His mother was most astonished to see him there, with the dry bread beside him, when she came home.

"Oh, Ma!" wept Goofy, "I lost that hanky, I did, I did! Though it was pinned on me, too! So I've emptied my money-box, and got myself some bread and put myself to bed."

"But, Goofy," said his mother, puzzled, "what's that on your head?"

Goofy put up his hand to his head. He had quite forgotten that he had made himself a sunhat out of his hanky! He

pulled it off, and looked at it joyfully, very
red in the face.

"Oh, Ma! I didn't lose it! I can get up!
I can have my money back! I just made a
sunhat of my hanky and then forgot all
about it! Ma, I've been very, very silly."

"I could have told you that long ago,"
said his mother, laughing. "Get up
quickly, Goofy – there's the biggest slice
of fruit cake that ever you saw waiting on
the kitchen table for you!"

Well, well, well – some people do
peculiar things, don't they?

Mr Miggle's Spectacles

Once upon a time there was a gnome called Miggle. He thought a lot of himself, and he hoped other people did too – but they didn't! They thought Mr Miggle was a fat, greedy, mean old gnome, who always pretended he was too poor to help anyone.

Mr Miggle was vain. He quite thought everyone liked him and admired him, but he did wish they would say so. Nobody ever told him he was good-looking, and nobody said he was kind or good.

"I suppose they are too shy to say so to me," he thought, as he walked proudly down the village street, dressed in a new yellow suit tied up with red ribbons all down the front. "How I wish I knew what everyone was thinking about me! It would be lovely to know. I expect they are thinking how fine I look, and what a grand gnome I am!"

Now it so happened that on that day a pedlar came to Mr Miggle's village, selling all kinds of strange things. He called at Mr Miggle's house after tea, and Mr Miggle looked at his things.

"Here's a broom that will sweep by itself," said the pedlar, showing Miggle a little yellow broom. "Or here's a jug which is always full of new milk."

"No, thanks," said Mr Miggle. "I don't want those."

"Well, what about a pair of spectacles that will tell you what everyone is thinking about you," said the pedlar, picking up a little red case. In it lay a pair of big, round spectacles with very peculiar glass that winked and blinked all the time.

"Ooh!" said Mr Miggle. "Just what I want! How much?"

"Three pieces of gold!" said the pedlar. "They are very rare, you know."

Mr Miggle put the spectacles on and looked hard at the pedlar. The man immediately thought of something nice about Miggle, for he knew the gnome was reading his thoughts.

Mr Miggle saw what he thought – the pedlar was thinking: "What a nice gnome! I'm sure he will be sensible enough to buy my wonderful spectacles, for they are very cheap indeed!"

Mr Miggle wasn't clever enough to know that the pedlar was thinking these things on purpose, and he was very

pleased. He paid the gold without a word and the pedlar went off, chuckling to himself, thinking of the dreadful shocks that Miggle would have when he put the spectacles on and found out what people really thought of him!

Miggle was very excited. He could hardly sleep that night for thinking of the lovely time he would have the next day, finding out what everyone thought of him.

"I shall put on my new suit again," he said to himself. "I look nice in that. Then I will walk down the street with my spectacles on and see what everyone is thinking about me."

53

So the next morning he put on his fine yellow suit, popped his pointed hat on, and settled his new spectacles on his nose. Then out he went down the street.

The first person he met was old Dame Wimple. Miggle smiled at her and she nodded back. She didn't say a word. Miggle looked at her through his glasses to see what she was thinking – and my, what a shock he got!

"Silly, fat old gnome!" the old dame was thinking. "I suppose he thinks he looks fine in that awful suit. What a sight he looks!"

Miggle nearly cried out in horror. Could old Dame Wimple really be thinking that? No, no, the glasses must be making some mistake!

Round the corner he met Skip and Jump, the little boy pixies who lived at Hello Cottage. He smiled at them, and they said good morning to him most politely. Mr Miggle looked through his glasses to see what they were really thinking and again he got a most terrible shock.

"Nasty, mean old thing!" Skip was thinking. "He never gives a little pixie even a penny!"

"What an ugly face old Miggle's got!" Jump was thinking. "I should hate to meet him at night in a dark corner!"

Well! Miggle was so surprised that he stood quite still and stared at the two little pixies. They were frightened and ran away. Miggle heaved a great sigh and went on.

"I suppose children always think silly things like that," he said to himself. "It's no use taking any notice of them. It's the grown-ups that matter."

At the roadside stood a brownie, selling red apples. Mr Miggle looked at him through his glasses, hoping to see some really nice thoughts in his head. But, no, again he was disappointed.

"It's no use asking this mean-looking old gnome to buy my nice apples," the brownie was thinking. "He looks a real miser, although he is so fat."

Mr Miggle was shocked. Did he really look like a miser? He looked into a mirror set in a shop window. Yes, his mouth did look rather thin and mean. Oh dear, he wasn't having a very nice morning!

Ah, here came Mr Snoop, his friend. Now he would read some nice thoughts, surely. He shook hands with Snoop and looked at him through his glasses. Oh goodness! Mr Snoop was thinking no better thoughts than the others.

"So he's got a new suit again," Snoop was thinking. "Why does he always have

his suits so tight they look as if they were bursting? And why does Miggle eat so much? He really is much too fat. I'm sure I don't know why I'm friends with him. He's a mean, greedy fellow and I don't really like him at all."

Snoop was very much surprised to see Miggle burst into tears and hurry down the street without a word. He had no idea that the fat little gnome could see what he was thinking and had been very much upset by it.

"Well, well," thought Snoop, "what next? He really is a silly chap, that Miggle."

Miggle dried his eyes under his glasses and walked up the hill towards Mrs Lemon's cottage. Mrs Lemon was out in her garden watering her flowers. Miggle hardly dared to look at her in case he read something horrid about himself.

"But she's the kindest person in the village," he thought. "So she's sure to be thinking something nice about me. I'll see if she is."

He said good morning to Mrs Lemon

and read her thoughts. Poor Miggle! He had no luck that morning, for Mrs Lemon, kind-hearted as she was, was not thinking very nice things about the foolish, fat gnome.

"Here comes old greedy Miggle," she was thinking. "Poor old fellow! I wonder if he guesses how everyone laughs at him and dislikes him. I believe he thinks we all like him. If only he knew what we think, he would get a dreadful shock!"

Miggle did get a dreadful shock! He looked at Mrs Lemon as if he couldn't believe his ears and eyes. She was astonished.

"What's the matter?" she asked. "Are you ill? Come into my garden and sit down for a bit."

Mr Miggle read what she was thinking.

"Miggle looks ill," she was thinking. "I suppose as usual he's been eating too much. What a dreadful fellow he is, to be sure."

Miggle stopped at the gate and spoke sadly to Mrs Lemon.

"I can see what you are thinking, Lucy Lemon," he said. "I have magic spectacles on. You have been thinking I am a greedy fellow, whom nobody likes. Ah well, perhaps you are right."

Mrs Lemon was astonished. She looked at Miggle's spectacles and saw that they were magic ones. She was sorry for the unhappy gnome, for she knew what a lot of shocks he must have had that morning.

"Come in for a minute," she said kindly. "I didn't mean you to see my thoughts – but people can't very well help their thoughts, can they?"

Miggle came in and sat down on a

bench. He took off his glasses and looked at Mrs Lemon.

"Am I a very horrid fellow?" he asked.

"You are rather," said Mrs Lemon. "But you needn't be. If only you wouldn't think so much of yourself, Miggle, and would think a little more of other people, you'd be all right. And you shouldn't eat so much, you know – you're getting fat and ugly. You used to be such a good-looking gnome!"

Miggle was very sad.

"Do you think I could ever be nice?" he asked.

"It's never too late to mend," said Mrs Lemon. "You musn't blame other people for what they think of you, you know. It is you that have made their thoughts about you. The people in this village are kindly folk, and it's your own fault if they think unkindly about you. What about trying to turn over a new leaf, Miggle? Try for a month and then put the magic glasses on again!"

Miggle said he would try. He put his glasses into their case, thanked Mrs Lemon for helping him and went sadly home. He sat down by his fire and made all sorts of plans.

He wouldn't be so greedy. He would take good long walks each day to make himself thinner. He would be kind and generous to the children and to the poor people. He would ask Snoop, his friend, to help him.

Poor Mr Miggle! He tried hard for a month and it wasn't easy. Snoop and Mrs Miggle helped him, and at last he really felt a bit different. He looked for his magic glasses to put on to see if people

were thinking kinder thoughts about him – and they weren't there!

He had lost them, so he never knew what other people were thinking about him after all – but as he really is different, I expect their thoughts are different, too. Don't you?

Nobody knows where those glasses went to. If you should ever come across them, what sort of thoughts would you read in other people's minds if you put those spectacles on? I wonder!

The
Roundabout Man

The fair had come to the town. It was in the big field at one end of the town, and the children eagerly watched all the tents being put up, and the swings and hoopla, and oh, the big roundabout!

It was a most magnificent roundabout. There were animals to ride on, and these animals went up and down as well as round and round.

"It's just the nicest kind of roundabout there is," said all the children.

"If I went on, I'd ride the camel," said Judy to her twin, Jane. "What would you ride, Jane?"

"That lovely swan," said Jane. "Then I should pretend I was sailing and flying at the same time, going up and down, up and down, and round and round."

"It's a pity Mummy's ill in hospital," said Judy. "She'd give us some money and let us go to the fair. But Auntie Nina won't, I'm sure. She never gives us anything, even when we run lots of errands for her."

Auntie Nina did not believe in giving a lot of money to children. She believed in them paying for things themselves, and saving up if they wanted anything.

"You have your pocket money," she said, "and that should be enough. If you want anything, you must save up for it."

So when Judy and Jane asked if they might go to the fair, and please could

they have the money, Auntie Nina said, "What about your pocket money? That is given to you to spend on things like the fair."

"Well, Auntie," said Judy, "we haven't got any money at all till this Saturday, and then we want to spend it on something else."

Judy and Jane had spent their pocket money on buying flowers to take to their mother in hospital, and they each wanted to take her a bunch of primroses that week. But that meant there wouldn't be even a penny left.

Auntie Nina shook her head. "I can't give you any more money," she said. "I'm sorry. I don't believe in handing out money to children whenever they ask for it. You have plenty of pocket money. If you can't save it up, you must go without things you want!"

There was no more to be said. Judy and Jane turned away sadly. Now they wouldn't go to the fair, and they would never ride on that lovely roundabout.

"I wouldn't mind not doing anything

else at the fair, if only we could ride on the roundabout," Judy said that evening, as they peeped over the hedge and watched the lions, tigers, swans, camels and bears going round and round and round to the sound of merry music. "I just love that roundabout!"

They were on an errand for Auntie Nina. They had to go all the way to the farm for some eggs. It was a long way, and they had to be home for supper, so they couldn't stop long to watch the fair. They soon ran off, and made their way over the fields to the farm.

When they got there, the farmer's wife gave them the eggs and some hot biscuits from her oven. While they were eating them, a little old lady came into the farmhouse kitchen.

"Are you children going back to the town now?" she asked.

"Yes, we are," said Judy.

"Well, then, I wonder if you'd take this parcel to my son for me," said the old lady. "It's his washing. He wants clean

things for tomorrow, and I haven't been able to get out today because my legs have been bad. Could you take it for me, do you think? His lodgings are at the end of the High Street."

Oh dear! That was a long way to go. They might be late for supper, too, and Auntie Nina would be angry. Still, they must help the old lady, and if they ran all the way they could do it.

So the twins took the parcel of washing and went. They ran all the way, panting, taking it in turns to carry the parcel, which was quite heavy.

When they got to the house in the High Street there was nobody in! They rang the bell and knocked loudly but no one came. The woman next door put her head out of the window and called to them. "Who do you want?"

The twins looked at the name written on the parcel. "We've got a parcel for Mr Tom Taylor," said Jane.

"Oh, him! Well, you'll find him at the fair," said the woman. "I think he's with the swings."

"Shall we take the parcel to him?" wondered Judy. "Yes, we'd better. We can't leave it here on the doorstep!"

So they rushed off to the fairground. At the gate they said they had a parcel for Mr Tom Taylor, of the swings.

"Tom? Oh, he's the roundabout man," said the woman at the gate. "Over there, look. That man with the curly black hair."

The twins went up to the curly-haired man. "Well, do you want a ride?" he said.

"No," said Judy. "We've just brought you your washing. We went to the farm where your mother is staying, to get some eggs, and she asked us to bring you this parcel. But when we went to your lodgings there was nobody in, so we brought it to you here."

"Well, what kind children!" said Mr Taylor. "Who would have thought there were children who'd do a nice thing like that for a roundabout man! Wait a minute. I'll give you a pound for your kindness."

"Oh, no thank you," said Judy at once.

70

"We did it to help your mother. Our mother doesn't like us to take money for things like that."

"Well, well, so you've got a mother as nice as yourself, have you?" said the roundabout man, putting the pound back in his pocket. "But look here – you musn't be the only people doing a kindness. I like being kind too, you know. Have you been on my roundabout?"

"No, never," said the twins.

71

"Well, have a ride now," said the roundabout man. "Go on! Choose what animal you like!"

"We'd love to," said Jane, looking longingly at the roundabout, which had just stopped. "But we are awfully late. Our auntie, who's looking after us, will be cross if we aren't back for supper. We'll have to go."

"You come back tomorrow," said the roundabout man. "Now, I won't take no for an answer! Will you promise me to come back tomorrow, and choose an animal to ride on?"

"Oh, we'd love to!" said the twins, joyfully. "Thank you so much!"

They ran home, and were only just in time for supper. When they told their aunt all that had happened she was pleased.

"Well, if you want to go and get your little reward, you can go," she said. "You were very good children to refuse the pound he offered, and to come home without a ride so that you wouldn't be late. You deserve a treat. And why didn't you tell me you were spending all your pocket money on flowers for your mother? If I'd known that I would have given you some for the fair!"

Well, the next day Auntie Nina gave them a whole pound each, and off they went, full of delight.

They paid to go in, and when they got

to the roundabout the curly-haired man greeted them joyously.

"Here you are then! I've been waiting for you. I'm going to let the roundabout have a very, very long go, just for you. Choose your animal, please."

"We can pay for our ride after all," said Judy. "We've each got some money."

"Now, look here!" said the roundabout man. "Fair's fair! Did you let me pay you for your bit of kindness yesterday? No, you didn't. Then I shan't allow you to pay me for mine. Choose your animal."

So Judy chose the camel she wanted and Jane chose the swan. The music began, the roundabout started to move. Up and down, up and down, went the camel and the swan, and round and round and round.

It was the very longest roundabout ride that anyone had ever known. I wish I'd been on it, too, don't you? I'd have chosen the lion, I think. What would you have had?

Poor Bunny's Whiskers

There was once a white bunny who had lovely black whiskers. They stuck out each side of his nose and made him look very smart. He was very proud of them.

He was called Whisker-Bunny by all the other toys, and he did like his name. He used to pull his whiskers out straight every night and see that they were tidy before he went to play. You can't think how proud he was of them!

And then, one day, what do you think happened? The little girl he lived with, Anne-Marie, asked her cousin to stay with her for two nights – and the very first day Cousin Janet came she pulled out all the bunny's whiskers!

Wasn't it dreadful? Janet picked up the bunny and looked at him. Then she said, "I don't like his whiskers, Anne-Marie. I shall pull them out."

"You musn't," said Anne-Marie. "He wouldn't like it."

"He's only a toy," said Janet, and she pulled out one whisker.

"He's a darling toy, and I love him," said Anne-Marie crossly. "Don't do that, Janet!"

"I shall then," said Janet, and she pulled out another black whisker. Poor Whisker-Bunny could have cried – but as it was daytime he couldn't say a word!

"Janet, I shall tell Mummy!" said Anne-Marie.

"And she will say, 'Don't tell tales,'" said Janet.

Anne-Marie knew that was true. So she couldn't do anything at all, because Janet was bigger than she was and if she tried to snatch Whisker-Bunny away from her, one of his legs might come off, and that would be worse than whiskers.

"There! All his whiskers are off now!" said Janet.

So they were. He looked strange without his fine black whiskers – just a little white-faced bunny with a soft nose and no whiskers in his cheeks at all.

That night the poor bunny wept and wept. "I can't be called Whisker-Bunny any more!" he sobbed. "I look so funny – not like myself. I don't think I am myself. I've always been Whisker-Bunny and now I'm not. Who am I? Oh, I am so unhappy!"

The brown teddy put his arms round him and comforted him. The monkey looked fierce and so did the sailor doll. Nobody liked Janet. She didn't love toys. She just picked them to pieces. She had

no love or kindness in her, as Anne-Marie
had.

The sailor doll thought hard. How
could they give Whisker-Bunny more
whiskers? They had all seen Mother
sweep the other whiskers up in the
carpet-sweeper, and now they would be in
the dustbin. So any whiskers would have
to be new ones.

"I'm so miserable," sobbed Whisker-
Bunny, crying tears all down the teddy
bear's brown fur. "I do want some
whiskers!"

What could he have for whiskers?

Where could any be found? Everyone thought and thought – but the only black thing that the sailor doll could think of was Janet's own black curly hair!

"Aha! Oho!" the sailor doll cried suddenly, jigging up and down in excitement. "I have an idea! As it was Janet who took away the bunny's whiskers she should give him his new ones!"

"How?" said all the toys in surprise.

"Well, we'll go and pull out some of her black hairs!" said the sailor doll. "They would make beautiful whiskers!"

"But it would hurt her," said the baby doll.

"And why not?" said the teddy bear, wiping the bunny's tears off his own fur. "She hurts other people. Let her feel what it's like! Come on, everyone!"

All the toys trooped out of the playroom into the next room, where Janet and Anne-Marie were asleep. The sailor doll hopped up to the pillow. He took hold of one of Janet's curly hairs and gave a tug!

"Ooh!" said Janet, and woke up. Then she rubbed her head and went to sleep again. The sailor doll pulled two more hairs out. Janet woke again and rubbed her head hard. It hurt. When she was asleep once more the sailor doll chose four or five fine long hairs and tugged them out.

"Ooh!" said Janet and woke up in a fright. "What's the matter with my head!"

Then she saw the sailor doll with his handful of hair!

"How dare you pull out my hair!" she said in a rage.

"You pulled out the bunny's whiskers," said the sailor doll. "Serves you right!"

He slipped off the bed. All the toys ran back to the playroom, chuckling. They had done to Janet what she had done to the bunny. The teddy got a needle from the workbasket and threaded a hair. In no time he had sewn it through the bunny's cheeks. A long piece stuck out each side and made a wonderful pair of whiskers, quite curly! All the toys shrieked in delight. Again the bear threaded the needle, and very soon the bunny had about eight pairs of fine black curly whiskers in his cheeks. The toys crowded round him admiringly.

"Whisker-Bunny, you look beautiful!" said the baby doll.

"Whisker-Bunny, you are simply splendid," said the teddy bear.

"Whisker-Bunny, your whiskers are finer than ever!" said the monkey.

Whisker-Bunny was so pleased. He looked at himself in the mirror on the

wall of the doll's-house, and he really did think he looked fine. He thanked the teddy bear and the sailor doll for all their trouble, and looked as happy as could be.

"Dear Whisker-Bunny, it's nice to see you smiling!" said all the toys.

In the morning, what a surprise for Anne-Marie! When she picked up the bunny, there he was with a marvellous collection of curly black whiskers.

"Where did you get them from?" Anne-Marie cried in delight. "Look, Janet, Whisker-Bunny has new whiskers."

Janet looked – and as soon as she saw those whiskers she knew what they were! She guessed at once!

"Janet, where could Whisker-Bunny have got new whiskers?" said Anne-Marie.

Janet wouldn't answer. She went very red and turned away. She didn't tell anyone at all where those whiskers came from. So if ever you meet Anne-Marie, you'll be able to tell her! As for Janet, she has been much kinder to her toys since then. I'm not surprised – are you?

Matilda Screams the House Down!

There was once a little girl who screamed whenever things went wrong. My goodness, how she screamed! She made everybody jump, and the cat and dog flew behind the sofa in fright. The people next door shut their windows, and passers-by wondered whatever was the matter.

"I don't know what to do with Matilda," said her mother. "If I punish her for screaming, she only screams more loudly. If I take no notice at all, she screams until I do. And if I give her what she is screaming for, she makes up her mind to scream next time. Oh dear, oh dear!"

Now one day when Matilda was screaming, a little band of brownies passed by. When they heard the dreadful screams their hair stood on end and they trembled with fright. Then one of them peeped in at the window and saw that it was only Matilda, sitting on the floor kicking her heels on the carpet, screaming for all she was worth!

"I want an ice cream!" screamed Matilda, and she yelled and howled till the cat jumped up the chimney in fright.

"You naughty girl," said Bron, the chief brownie, looking in at the window. "You very naughty girl! You'll scream the place down one day."

Matilda looked at him angrily. "I wish I could!" she said. "I'd like to scream the house down. Then perhaps my mummy would give me a strawberry ice cream."

Bron turned to his little men. "She says she'd like to scream the place down," he said, with a grin. "Shall we take her to Tumbledown Land and let her try?"

"Yes!" they shouted, putting their hands over their ears, for Matilda had started again. Into the house they swarmed, caught hold of Matilda by the hair, the hands, and her dress, and

hurried her, still screaming, out of the window. Matilda was most surprised. She struggled. She wriggled. It was no good at all. She simply had to go with those little brownies!

They hurried her down the road and into a lane she never remembered seeing before. Into a wood she went and out the other side – and there she was, in funny Tumbledown Land!

There were strange-looking houses everywhere, all crooked and leaning over as if they must fall at any moment. There were sheds just hanging together by a few nails. It was a funny-looking place.

"Now, Matilda," said Bron pleasantly, "you can scream the place down. Go into this house to begin with."

He took her into a tumbledown place, and the little men sat her on the floor with a bump. Matilda was very angry indeed. She opened her big mouth and screamed at the top of her voice. My, how she screamed!

And she screamed the place down – yes, she really did! The whole house came tumbling down round her with a crash and bang! My goodness, Matilda was

startled! She stopped screaming for a moment and looked at all the mess. A bit of brick hit her on her head and hurt her. She screamed again. Down fell another bit of the house, and soon it was all in pieces around her, and dust was flying about everywhere! Matilda was really frightened.

Bron peeped round the mess. "Good!" he said. "You screamed that place down beautifully, didn't you! Now come and do another."

Poor Matilda was dragged into an old smelly shed and dumped on the floor again. She was very angry, so she opened her mouth and let out such a piercing yell that even the brownies jumped in alarm.

Down fell the shed at once! Not a bit of it was left! A small board fell on Matilda's leg and she screamed in pain. The brownies pulled her up at once.

"Don't waste your screams!" they said. "This is fun to watch. Come and scream another place down!"

And into a bigger house they pushed

the angry little girl, still yelling and screaming. The house began to fall down at once. Matilda was afraid she would be hurt and she tried to get out but the brownies pushed her back.

"No, don't come out yet," they said. "You haven't screamed the place down, Matilda. Scream!"

"I shan't," said the little girl, and she shut her mouth firmly.

"Your mother won't give you any ice creams," said Bron suddenly, and of course Matilda at once screamed in anger. And down came the house, *crash-smash-bang-clang*! Matilda rushed out in fright and she actually remembered that she had better not scream in case she brought down a chimney on top of her!

"Take me home – oh, take me home," begged Matilda. "I don't like this. I don't like screaming the place down."

"Well, if you're sure you're not going to scream any more just now, I suppose the fun is over," said Bron. "But look here, Matilda, we'll be along the next time you scream, and we'll let you scream a few

more places down for us. It's such fun to watch!"

Matilda pursed up her mouth and didn't say a word. If those little men thought she was going to scream any more places down for them, they were mistaken, Matilda thought to herself. Good gracious! She might have been badly hurt.

She was taken home. Her mother popped her head in the room and saw Matilda playing quietly with her toys. "I'm just going out to the town," she said to Matilda. "I won't be long."

"I want to come too," said Matilda. But her mother said no. Matilda was just going to open her mouth and scream when she remembered those little men. She shut her mouth firmly. She was not going to scream any more places down – and, dear me, how dreadful it would be if she screamed her own house down around her ears. That would never do!

Her mother was surprised that Matilda didn't scream as usual – but she was even more surprised as the days went by and Matilda screamed no more. How pleased everybody was – but nobody knew why Matilda was suddenly so good.

But I know and so do you! And if you know a screamer, just give them this story to read, will you? It would be fun to take them to Tumbledown Land and see them screaming a few houses down round their heads, wouldn't it?

Something Funny
Going On

"Mrs Jones – we're going away for a week," said Peter and Julie's mother to the plump little woman who came to help her each day. "We shall lock up the house; but I wonder if you'd mind feeding Whiskers for us?"

"Feed your dear old cat – of course I will!" said Mrs Jones. "It'll be a pleasure. I'll fetch fish from the shop and cook it myself for old Whiskers, and if you'll tell the milkman to leave some milk for him, I'll give him that, too. It won't take me more than a few minutes to pop across here and see to him."

"Oh, thank you – you're kind!" said Peter. "Whiskers will be quite all right then. He's got his box in the little summerhouse, with his blanket."

"He will be pleased to see you each day," said Julie. "Oh, I'm so glad you'll feed him. I'd quite made up my mind not to go away, if we couldn't get someone to look after him. Mummy, you'd have let me stay at home with him, wouldn't you?"

"No!" said Mother. "You couldn't leave old Whiskers without someone to look after him – and I couldn't leave you here all alone! Anyway, he'll be all right now. He loves Mrs Jones."

So the family said goodbye to Whiskers and went away quite happily. He didn't like them going, but he knew they would come back. They always did. He went to see if his comfortable little box was in the summerhouse. Yes, it was – and his blanket, too. Now he would be quite all right!

Mrs Jones kept her word. She brought a plate of fish each day, and poured out some milk for Whiskers as well. She had a quick look round the outside of the house to make sure that everything was all right.

On the third day she fed Whiskers as usual, and then hurried down the garden path to go home. She had to pass a little shed on the way, where the children's father kept his pots and tools and brooms and other gardening things. She was almost past the shed, when she suddenly stopped.

Had she heard something as she passed the shed? Surely she had! She went back a little and listened. Was that a noise inside, or wasn't it? She bent down and looked through the keyhole. But it was dark in the shed and she could see nothing.

But she heard something as she bent down and peeped. She heard a kind of scraping noise, she was sure she did! And then she heard a little rattling sound. After that there was silence.

"Well – I suppose it was a mouse!" she said and called down the garden to Whiskers. "There's a mouse in here, Whiskers. You'd better come and sit by the door and scare him!" Then away she went home.

Next day Mrs Jones fed Whiskers again and petted him as she always did. He was very fond of her and rubbed himself against her legs, purring loudly.

"Well, I must go," she said, and went back over the lawn. She suddenly remembered the noises she had heard in the shed the day before, and went close to it. And dear me, what a strange thing, she heard noises in there again!

Scrape-scrape! Rattle-rattle! And then she distinctly heard a little hissing noise.

"Bless us all – surely it can't be a snake in there!" she thought. "No – of course not! It must have been the wind hissing through a crack. Oh, lands sake – what's that now?"

She listened. It sounded as if a lot of little things were falling down – wooden seed labels perhaps? But who was in there playing about? Could it be someone hiding in the shed?

Crash! That was quite a big noise! Mrs Jones jumped and then, feeling quite shaky, bent down and looked through the keyhole again. What had fallen down?

"Must have been a little plant-pot," she thought, as she saw some bits and pieces on the floor of the shed. "This is strange. Who's in there, messing about?

I think I'll tell the police. Yes, I really think I will. If someone's hiding there, they may be waiting to burgle the house at night."

So she looked out for the tall policeman whose beat was near-by, and when she saw him she went up to him.

"Excuse me, but could you just come and have a look inside the shed in the garden of Red Chimneys?" she said. "The people are away and I feed the cat each day – and it's my belief there's someone hiding in their shed! Such noises going on – scrapings and rattling and crashings!"

"Really?" said the policeman. "Well, I'll go and investigate right now. Come on." So back they went to the house, and round to the shed. "It's locked," said the policeman, pulling at the door. "Ah – is that a key?"

"Dear me, yes," said Mrs Jones, staring at a big key hanging on a nail at the side of the shed. "I never noticed that before. Well – if the key's there, and the shed's locked, there can't be anyone inside, can there?"

Crash! A noise came from the shed just as she said that, and they both jumped. "There *is* someone there!" said the policeman. "Come on – I'll unlock the door and go in and have a look."

So he unlocked the door and flung it open. "Come on out, you!" he said, sternly. "And just tell me what you're doing there!"

But nobody came out. Not a single sound came from the shed! The policeman looked inside. It was quite a

small shed and there wasn't anywhere for a person to hide. How strange!

"Nobody there, Mrs Jones," he said, and went in at the door.

Crash! Something fell just beside him! He turned at once. A small box lay on the floor, and nails were flung around it, upset in the fall. The policeman stared at them in surprise.

"I don't like it," said Mrs Jones, in a shaky voice. "I really don't. Who threw that box of nails at you, Mr Policeman? There's nobody here."

"It seemed to come from above my head," said the policeman. "Ah, wait – look! That little flowerpot up there is moving – down it comes! Well, I'm blessed! What is going on here? That almost hit my helmet!"

"You be careful," said Mrs Jones. "There's funny goings-on here. Oooh – there's that hissing again."

Sss-sss-ssss! Yes, there was certainly a hissing noise! It came from the top shelf. The policeman saw an old chair and stood on it. He looked on the crowded

top shelf – and then he jumped as a small head with bright eyes peered over at him.

"What is it, what is it?" cried Mrs Jones.

"Well, bless us all – if it isn't a tortoise!" said the policeman, and he began to laugh. "Tortoises can hiss, you know, and see, here's the box it must have been put into for its winter sleep! It woke up because the weather turned so warm, and wandered out of its box along this shelf."

"Knocking things over!" said Mrs Jones. "Well I never! I am sorry I called you here just for a tortoise, Mr Policeman!"

"Well, I won't arrest him!" said the policeman with a chuckle. "And you were quite right to report to me. I'll just lock this shed and get out on my beat again."

"No – leave it for a minute," said Mrs Jones. "The tortoise will want water to drink and a bit of lettuce to eat. It belongs to Peter and Julie, you know. Well, well – so you weren't a burglar hiding here, old Shelly-Back. You rascal you, tipping things down on the policeman! You wait till I tell the children of your little tricks!"

They did laugh when she told them. "Thank you for looking after Whiskers for us," said Julie. "Look, we've brought back a present for you – a china cat just like Whiskers."

"And tomorrow I shall buy you a china tortoise to go with the cat!" said Peter. "Because you've been so kind to them both."

Mrs Jones has them on her chimney-piece to this day – and when she told me how it was they had been given to her, I really thought I must tell you, too!

The Tippitty Bird's Feather

Nobbly the gnome had a tippitty bird's feather and he was very proud of it. It was bright green with yellow spots and a purple patch at the tip. Anyone who had a tippitty bird's feather was lucky, so you may be sure Nobbly kept it safe.

His Aunt Jerusha had sent it to him as a birthday present. He showed it to Higgle and Rikky and Winks, who lived with him.

"See my tippitty feather?" he said. "Well, that will bring me luck. I don't mind lending it to you sometimes, but whoever uses it must put it back into that tall red vase on the mantelpiece, without fail."

"We promise to do that," said Higgle, Rikky and Winks, and they kept their promise and always put the tippitty feather back in the tall red vase.

Now, one day Nobbly felt that he wanted a bit of good luck, so he went to the tall red vase to take out the feather. But it wasn't there!

"Bother!" said Nobbly. "Now, who's had my tippitty feather and not put it back? I shall be very, very angry with Higgle, Rikky or Winks, whoever has got it."

He shouted for them. "Higgle! Rikky! Winks! Come here at once."

They came running. Nobbly pointed to the tall red vase. "Where's my tippitty feather?" he demanded. "Who has got it? I shall be very cross with whichever of you has forgotten to put it back into the red vase."

Higgle, Rikky and Winks looked at one another in dismay. Nobbly could get very cross. Who could have got the feather?

"Higgle, you borrowed it on Thursday to stir the cream!" said Rikky. "What did you do with it after that? Did you leave it in the cream jug?"

They went to look. No, it wasn't there. Then Winks remembered something. "Rikky, you wanted a pen to write with, and there wasn't one, so you took the feather out of the cream jug, sharpened the end, and wrote a letter with it. Don't you remember?" he said.

"Oh yes," said Rikky. "Well, perhaps I left it on the writing-desk."

But it wasn't there either. Then Higgle remembered something else. "Nobbly," he said. "You wanted to play bows and arrows, and you took the feather from the writing-desk, and used it for an arrow. Don't you remember?"

"Yes, I remember," said Nobbly, "but Rikky came and borrowed it after that to clean his big pipe with. I remember telling him it was a silly thing to do with a nice feather like the tippitty one."

"Oh yes – I did take it to clean my pipe," said Rikky, "but it was too big to go into the stem of my pipe, so I didn't use it after all. But I might have left it by my pipe."

No, it wasn't there. Higgle, Rikky and Winks frowned and tried to remember what happened to it next.

"Oh, I know!" said Winks, "the teapot spout got stuck up, don't you remember, yesterday teatime, and we got the feather to clean it. We poked out a whole lot of big tea-leaves that had got stuck."

"So we did," said Higgle and Winks. "But what happened after that? It's not in the teapot now."

They all frowned again, and Nobbly began to look angry. Really, the things people did with his lucky tippitty feather!

"I know! Higgle borrowed it after tea yesterday to get some boiled sweets out of the jar," said Winks. "Don't you remember – they had stuck together, and Higgle said the sharp point of the tippitty feather would force the sweets apart."

"And we got it to put in the sweet jar!" cried Rikky. "Yes – and maybe it's there still."

But, no, it wasn't. It was really very peculiar that it had vanished like that. Nobbly frowned like a thunderstorm.

"Fancy using my feather for things like that!" he shouted. "I won't live with people like you! No, I won't. I shall go away and live with my Aunt Jerusha. Then you'll miss me and be sorry."

He rushed out of the room. They heard him take down his coat in the hall and fling it on. They heard him snatch his stick up. Then he stamped down the hall and opened the front door. He slammed it so hard that the tall red vase almost jumped off the mantelpiece.

Higgle, Rikky and Winks were full of dismay. They were fond of Nobbly. He couldn't go off like this! No, he really, really couldn't.

They rushed to the window. They saw Nobbly walking to the front gate, his hat and coat on and his stick swinging.

And then Higgle, Rikky and Winks gave a shout all together:

"Hey! Nobbly! Wait a minute!"

Nobbly stopped. "What's the matter? Have you found my tippitty feather?"

"Yes! We know where it is!" yelled the three, and they tore out into the garden. Higgle whipped Nobbly's hat off his head with a yell.

"Here's the tippitty feather, you great

big silly! You put it in your hat yourself,
don't you remember? You took it out of
the vase this morning and stuck it in
your hat and said, 'I'm paying a call on
Dame Trim today and I'd like to look
smart.'"

Sure enough, there was the tippitty feather in Nobbly's hat. Nobbly looked at it. He went very red indeed. He looked at the others.

"I'm sorry," he said. "I'm very, very, very, very, very . . ."

"It's all right," said Higgle, Rikky and Winks, putting their arms round him. "Come back and have some lemonade, silly. Higgle has just made some."

"And bring that tippitty feather with you," said Higgle, with a grin, "because I've a sort of feeling that the lemonade wants stirring, and we might use the feather for that!"

He Wouldn't Wipe
His Shoes

Keith was always getting into trouble because he wouldn't wipe his shoes. He would go out into the garden to play, and then come straight in without wiping his feet even once on the mat.

So he left muddy marks on the carpet, and you could always see where he had walked in the house because there was mud everywhere! He really was naughty.

"Wipe your feet, Keith!" his mother said each time he came in.

"Wipe your feet, Keith," his aunt said when he went to see her on Saturdays.

"Wipe your feet, Keith," his teacher said to him each day at school.

But did he wipe his feet? No, not if he could possibly slip indoors without doing so! And even when he did wipe them, it was what his mother called a lick and a promise!

Now one day Keith and the other children in his class were told that there was to be a match between the five classes to see who could win the most marks for good manners. The teachers wanted to find out which was the best-mannered class, and all the children were told they could win marks for their own class by trying hard.

"What sort of manners will count for marks?" asked Harry.

"Well," said the teacher, "all good manners will count, Harry. Boys raise their caps to ladies – that is good manners. Children give up their seats to grown-ups in buses or trains – that is good manners. Saying please and thank you – standing back for others to pass – opening doors for grown-ups – never pushing – wiping your shoes – shutting the door quietly behind you – all these things are good manners, and you can win marks for them this week."

"Suppose we don't do something we

should? What then?" asked Harry.

"Well, I'm afraid bad manners will make you lose a mark!" said the teacher. Harry gazed round at Keith.

"Ha!" he said. "I guess you'll make us lose all the marks we earn by forgetting to wipe your feet every time you come in, Keith. Bother you!"

Keith went red. "I'll try to remember," he said.

He did try – but he had forgotten for so long that he really couldn't remember even when he tried! So he lost a great many marks each day for the class, and they were very cross.

"It's too bad of you," said Harry to Keith at the end of the week. "Our class is bottom for good manners! And it's all because you kept losing us marks for not wiping your feet. Horrid boy!"

Keith was unhappy. How dreadful to try hard over something and still not be able to remember! He ran home, wondering how he could cure himself.

That afternoon his mother sent him to the cobbler's with a pair of shoes to be mended. The cobbler was a little man, bent double over his shoe-making, and he was so old that he had even forgotten himself how old he was. Keith thought he must be about a hundred.

"Good afternoon, little man," he said to Keith, peering at him from behind thick glasses. "And how's the world using you?"

"Not very well," said Keith, and he told the cobbler how he had made his class bottom for the week, all because he simply could not remember to wipe his feet when he came in.

"Very bad, very bad," said the old

cobbler. "Don't you know that damp mud is bad for shoes? Ah, you should take care of shoes, my boy. If you had made as many as I had, of good stout leather, you would be very careful of them, yes you would. Now, I remember when I was a lad, my brother was the same as you – never wiped his shoes once. Ah, but he was cured!"

"Was he?" asked Keith. "How was he cured? Could I be cured too?"

"Yes, for sure!" said the old man, and he chuckled like a hen clucking. "Now see, young man – take this tin home, and clean your shoes with this bit of yellow polish I put inside. Clean all your outdoor

shoes with it, and I tell you, you'll soon be cured, just as my brother was. Ho-ho-ho! He was cured all right!"

But he wouldn't tell Keith how, and the boy ran home with the tin of yellow polish, wondering whatever cure it could be. He didn't really like to try it – but at last, thinking that it couldn't possibly hurt him, he took all his outdoor shoes and boots, found a shoe brush, and set to work to polish his shoes with the yellow polish.

His shoes shone brilliantly. It was marvellous polish. Keith slipped on his outdoor boots and went to afternoon school. Of course, he quite forgot to wipe his feet as usual. In he went, stepping on the mat, but not rubbing his feet at all.

He was a bit late. He took his place, and found his book – and then he noticed that his feet were beginning to feel dreadfully uncomfortable. His boots seemed to be growing smaller and smaller, tighter and tighter. At last poor Keith couldn't bear them on his feet! He

undid the laces and took off his muddy
boots, hoping that the master would not
see him.

And what do you think happened?
Why, as soon as his boots were off, they
ran over to the mat by themselves,
making a tremendous clatter! When they
got to the mat, they wiped themselves
thoroughly, scraping all the mud off as
carefully as could be!

Every one looked up when they heard
the clatter – and how they stared when
they saw Keith's big boots running over

to the mat, dragging their laces behind them. Then they began to laugh! How they laughed! Even the master laughed till the tears ran down his cheeks!

"Ho-ho-ho! Ha-ha-ha! Just look at those boots! Keith can't remember to wipe his own boots, so the boots are doing it for themselves! For shame, Keith! Ho-ho-ho!"

Keith went very red. He hated being laughed at. He sat looking very ashamed until his boots, now perfectly clean, came clattering back to him. He put them on. They seemed quite the right size now!

Every one was talking about the wonderful boots that Friday afternoon, but Keith didn't want to join in. He ran home and burst in at the door, longing to take off those dreadful boots! But as soon as he got in he saw his Uncle George there.

"Hello!" said Uncle George. "Here comes the thunderstorm!"

Keith ran to hug his uncle, for he was very fond of him. He quite forgot to wipe his feet, of course – but it wasn't very long before his boots reminded him!

They suddenly grew so tight that Keith almost squealed out. He undid the laces hurriedly – and, oh dear, those boots ran out of the room, all the way down the hall to the front-door mat, where they could be heard busily wiping the mud off the soles and heels!

"Goodness gracious me!" said Uncle

George, in the greatest astonishment.

"Well I never!" said Mother. And they both began to laugh till they cried! Keith didn't laugh. He felt very angry with himself.

Well, things went on like that all the weekend. It didn't matter which pair of outdoor boots or shoes Keith put on, they had all been polished with the yellow polish, and they each ran off to the mat to wipe themselves if Keith forgot – which he usually did!

By the time he got back to school on Monday the word had gone round that there was something very exciting about Keith's shoes, and all the boys and girls were longing to watch Keith forget to wipe his feet.

But for once Keith didn't forget! No – he really remembered, and he stood on the mat, wiping his feet just as all the others did. But poor Keith – he had left just a little bit of mud at the back of his left foot and the boot knew it all right. It grew tighter and tighter till Keith had to take it off – then away to the mat it ran, and wiped itself well till the tiny bit of mud had gone.

"This is dreadful!" thought Keith. "Not only have I got to remember to wipe my feet – but I've got to wipe every speck of mud off too! I shall never, never do it, and all my life I shall be laughed at because my boots and shoes run to the mat to wipe themselves. Oh, how I wish I had never told that old cobbler about myself!"

Well, the yellow polish lasted until Keith's feet grew too big for his boots. Then he had to have new ones, and he begged the cobbler not to rub any of his strange polish on them.

"Ah, but are you sure you're cured?" said the old man, with his clucking chuckle.

"Quite sure," said Keith firmly. "I haven't forgotten to wipe my feet for ages, and I'm sure I never shall again. So please let me have my new boots and shoes without any yellow polish at all."

"Very well," said the cobbler, and he kept his word. Keith's new boots and shoes were the same as yours and mine, and so far Keith has not once forgotten to wipe his feet on the mat.

His mother has still got his old boots and shoes, and she says she is waiting to give them to any boy or girl who has a bad memory for wiping feet!

Mother Hubbard's Honey

Mother Hubbard kept bees, and they made lovely golden honey for her. Mother Hubbard took it from the hives and put it into jars.

Then, for once, her cupboard was full when she went to it, instead of bare. Rows upon rows of honey jars stood there, waiting to be sold.

Now little Pixie Peep-About lived next door to Mother Hubbard, and he loved honey. But he wasn't a very good or very helpful pixie, so Mother Hubbard didn't give him any honey. She sold most of it, gave some to her friends, and kept six pots for herself.

Pixie Peep-About was cross because she never gave him any honey. "And I live next door, too!" he said to himself.

"She might give me just a taste. She knows I love honey."

But Peep-About never gave Mother Hubbard any of his gooseberries when they were ripe. And he didn't offer her an egg when his hens laid him plenty. So it wasn't surprising that he didn't get any honey.

One summer he watched Mother Hubbard's bees. "How busy they are," he said as he peeped over the wall. "In and out, in and out of those hives all the day long. And what is more, a lot of those

bees come into my garden and take the honey from my flowers!"

It was quite true. They did. But bees go anywhere and everywhere, so of course they went into Peep-About's garden too.

"Some of that honey they are storing in Mother Hubbard's hives is mine, taken from my flowers," thought Peep-About. "So Mother Hubbard ought to give me plenty!"

He told Mother Hubbard this, but she laughed. "Honey is free in the flowers," she said. "Don't be silly, Peep-About."

Now, one day Mother Hubbard went to take the honeycombs from her hives. They were beautiful combs, full of golden honey. She meant to separate the honey from the combs and store it in her jars. Peep-About knew she was going to do that. She did it every year.

"Now she'll have jars upon jars of honey, and she won't give me a single one," thought the pixie. "It's too bad. I haven't tasted honey for months, and I should love some on a bit of bread and butter."

Mother Hubbard poured the honey into her jars. She handed one to old Mr Potter, at the bottom of the garden. He was a kind old fellow and always gave Mother Hubbard tomatoes when he had some to spare. He was delighted.

"Look at that now," said Peep-About to himself. "Not a drop for me. Mean old thing! My, what delicious honey it looked."

The next day Mother Hubbard dressed herself up in her best, and set out to catch the bus, with three pots of honey in her basket. Peep-About met her as she went to the bus stop.

"Where are you going?" asked Peep-About.

"To see my sister, Dame Blue-Bonnet," said Mother Hubbard. "I'll be gone all day, so if you see the milkman, Peep-About, tell him to leave me a pint of milk."

"Gone all day," thought Peep-About. "Well, what about me getting in at the kitchen window, going to that cupboard, and helping myself to a few spoonfuls of honey!"

So, when Mother Hubbard was safely on the bus, Peep-About crept in at her kitchen window and went to the cupboard. It wasn't locked. He opened it and saw row upon row of jars of honey. Oh, what a lovely sight!

He was small and the cupboard was high. He tried to scramble up to one of the shelves and he upset a jar of honey. Down it went and poured all over him!

"Gracious!" said Peep-About in alarm. "It's all over me! How lovely it tastes!"

He thought he had better go back to his own home, scrape the honey off

himself, and eat it that way. So out of
the window he went.

But the garden was full of Mother
Hubbard's bees and they smelled the
honey on Peep-About at once.

"Zzzzzz! Honey! ZZZZZZ! Honey!"

they buzzed to one another, and flew round Peep-About. They tried to settle on the honey that was running down his head and neck.

"Go away! Go away! Stop buzzing round me!" he cried. But no matter how he beat them away, back they came again.

Peep-About had a terrible time, for wherever he went the bees went too. They followed him into his kitchen. They stung him when he flapped them away. They followed him out into the garden again. They followed him into the street. They wouldn't leave Peep-About alone for one minute.

He couldn't sit down and have his lunch. He had to go without his tea. He ran here and he ran there, but always the bees flew with him.

He had their honey on him, and they wanted it.

More and more bees came to join in the fun. At last Peep-About saw Mother Hubbard walking up her front path and he ran to her. She was astonished to see her bees round him in a big buzzing cloud.

"Take them away! Make them go to their hive!" wept Peep-About.

Mother Hubbard touched him and found he was sticky with honey. Then she knew what had happened.

"You went to steal some of my honey," she said sternly. "You're a bad pixie. You can keep the honey – and the bees too! I shan't call them off!"

So, until the bees went to bed in their hive that night, poor Peep-About had to put up with them. He ran for miles trying to get rid of them, but he couldn't. They could fly faster than he could run.

At last the bees went to bed. Peep-About stripped off his sticky suit and washed it. He got himself a meal. He cried all the time. "I shall never like honey again," he wept. "Never, never, never!"

The next day Mother Hubbard was sorry that she hadn't helped poor Peep-About, even though he had been a bad little pixie. So she sent him in a tiny jar of honey all for himself.

But wasn't it a pity – he couldn't eat it! He didn't like honey any more. He couldn't bear to look at it.

"It serves me right," he said. "When I couldn't have it, I loved it, and tried to take it. Now, here I've got a jar, and I can't bear to eat it. It's a good punishment for me, it really is!"

He was right. It was!

Mr Stamp-About
Goes Shopping

Mr Stamp-About stalked into Mr Tidy-the-Tailor's shop and banged on the counter.

"I want to be served!" he said. "I'm in a hurry!"

Mr Tidy turned from the customer he was serving. "Just a minute, sir," he said. "I'll come to you as soon as I've finished helping this gentleman."

"I want serving now," said Stamp-About, rudely.

"Very well, sir," said Mr Tidy, and called to the back of the shop. "Forward, please, Button!"

Out hurried a scared looking boy, with a button in one hand and a needle in the other. "I'm just sewing on those buttons, sir," he said. "Did you want me?"

133

"Yes. Serve this gentleman," said Mr Tidy, and poor little Button looked in alarm at the fierce Mr Stamp-About.

"I will not be served by this little shrimp!" said Mr Stamp-About, angrily.

"Well, sir – I haven't any lobsters serving in the shop today," said Mr Tidy, apologetically. That made his customer laugh loudly, and little Button giggled in delight.

Stamp-About stamped his foot, and began to roar. "I'm in a hurry! I've got to go to a grand luncheon party and I want a new coat and hat and umbrella – *at once!*"

"Show him some coats, Button," said Mr Tidy, and with trembling hands poor Button took down some coats from a rail.

Mr Stamp-About tried them on, grumbling all the time.

"Awful colour! Shocking pattern! What a collar! Look at these pockets! And the price – my word, what robbers you are here!"

"Well, would you like to fetch the policeman?" asked Mr Tidy, getting a bit tired of Stamp-About. "He's always interested in robbers. Look, he's just outside, across the street."

But Stamp-About didn't fetch him. He knew that the policeman wasn't very fond of him! He tried on more coats, and then called for hats.

"Silly hats! All too small!" he said.

"You have a rather a big head, sir," said Mr Tidy. "Look, there's a good hat, there. The largest size we have. Put it on his head, Button."

Button carefully fitted it on Stamp-About's head. It was just his size, and a very nice hat indeed.

"Hmm. Not bad," said Stamp-About, turning his head this way and that to see the hat better. "Yes, I'll have it, if it's not too much money. Now, what about an umbrella – and after that I'll decide on a coat."

Button gave him one. "Not bad," said Stamp-About and opened it so suddenly that Button fell over backwards. "Now where's that little shrimp gone? Hey! What are you squatting on the floor for? Get up at once!"

In the end Stamp-About chose a coat, a hat and an umbrella – but how he argued about the price! "If I buy three things I ought to have them cheap," he said, and began to stamp about the shop, calling Mr Tidy a robber and a thief until the poor man got so tired of him that he gave way. Anything to get Stamp-About out of his shop! He was scaring other customers away.

"Very well, I will take a pound off the price," said Mr Tidy. "Button, wrap up the things, then Mr Stamp-About can go."

"No, don't wrap them up," said Stamp-About. "I want to wear them. I told you I'm going to a grand luncheon party. Here's the money and I still think you're robbing me, charging so much even though you took a pound off the price."

Mr Tidy said nothing. He was sure he would lose his temper if he had much more of Stamp-About. Little Button tremblingly helped him into his new coat, and gave him the new hat and the new umbrella. Then he scampered into the

137

back of the shop, and sat down thankfully to his task of sewing on buttons.

Stamp-About went out of the shop without so much as a thank you. He muttered crossly as he went. "Robbers! What a price to pay for new clothes!"

He was on his way to Mr High-Up who was giving the party in his very grand house on the other side of the town. Stamp-About decided to take a short cut through the woods. Just then the wind got up and tugged at his hat, and he had to hold it on tightly.

"Stop it, wind!" he said. "Can't you see I'm wearing a new hat? I don't want it blown into the wood. Behave yourself!"

But the wind was going to do as it liked. It waited till Stamp-About was in the wood and then it pounced on him and blew his new hat right off his head, and what was more it blew it high up into a tree!

Stamp-About lost his temper and roared at the wind, and stamped round the tree. "How dare you! That's my new

hat! Blow it down to me at once! Shake
yourself, tree, and throw down my hat!"

But the hat didn't stir from the tree. It
hung up there on a small branch, and
jiggled a little in the wind.

"All right. I'll come up and get you,"
said Mr Stamp-About. "But I'd better
take off my grand new coat, else I shall
tear it on a branch. And I'll stand my
new umbrella beside it, too."

So he took off his coat and laid it
carefully on a tree-stump not far off. He
stood his umbrella beside it. Then back
he went to the tree and began to climb it.
It was a difficult tree to climb and little

bits and pieces kept catching at him as he climbed. He felt very cross indeed. What a long way up his hat was!

Just as he got almost to the hat, at the top of the tree, the wind pounced down again and blew so hard that the tree rocked from side to side. It made a loud rustling noise, and Stamp-About very nearly fell out. He clung to a bough for all he was worth.

Now, down in the wood below, was a little old man. He was very poor, and had come to pick up wood for his fire. He came up to the tree-stump where Stamp-About had put his coat and umbrella, and stared at them in surprise. Why were they there? Whose were they? Had someone left them there because he didn't want them any more? But the coat seemed a very good one – and the umbrella was a beauty!

"Does anyone own these?" shouted the old man. But nobody answered. Stamp-About was being blown about in the tree and he didn't hear a thing.

"Well, well, it seems a pity to leave

them here to rot in the wind and rain,"
said the old fellow. "I can sell them for
quite a bit of money."

So he picked them up and went off
with them, wearing the coat and
swinging the umbrella, feeling very
grand.

"Now who will buy these?" he thought.
"Yes, I'll go to old Tidy-the-Tailor's. He's
a nice fellow. He'll give me a fair price for
them."

But when he got to Mr Tidy's shop, the tailor was just going off to his lunch. He called to little Button. "Hey, Button, see to this man for me, will you? He says he's got second-hand clothes to sell. Give him a fair price." And off went Mr Tidy.

Button was astonished to see the coat and umbrella. "They can't be the ones I sold this morning, because that awful Mr Stamp-About went off in them," he thought. "And he certainly wouldn't give them away almost at once."

"Will you buy them?" asked the old fellow. "The coat is quite good, you know, and so is the umbrella."

"Yes, I know," said Button. "We sell the same things ourselves. I will give you half the price we charge when they are new. That's fair enough."

"Very fair!" said the old man, in delight. "Ah, I can see sausages for my supper every night this week and a fire in my kitchen and hot cocoa before I go to bed. That's what money means to me, young Button! I'll take it now."

He went off happily with the money, and jingled it in his pocket all the way to the sausage shop. What luck!

Button went back to his job of sewing on buttons but he hadn't been working for more than ten minutes when he heard a loud roaring outside the shop. Gracious, had a lion escaped from a circus? Button ran behind a rail of coats and trembled.

But it wasn't a lion. It was only a very, very angry Mr Stamp-About. He came stamping into the shop and roared for Mr Tidy.

"He's gone to his lunch," said Button, peering out fearfully from behind the coats. "There's only me here."

"Oh, the shrimp!" said Stamp-About, rudely. "Well, look here, someone's stolen that new coat and umbrella I bought this morning – the wind blew my hat up a tree and while I was climbing to fetch it, a thief came along and took my coat and umbrella."

Button immediately felt certain that the thief was the old man who had just sold him a coat and umbrella, and he was very frightened.

"Oh, sir," he began, "an old man came in just now and—"

"Don't interrupt me when I'm talking," said Stamp-About, angrily. "I tell you, when I came down the tree—"

"But, sir, I'm sure that the old man who—" said Button, earnestly, and once more Stamp-About cut him short, and even tried to box poor Button's ears.

"Stop talking about old men! Show me a coat exactly like the one I bought this morning, and an umbrella. I shall be ruined, having to buy them, but I simply must go well-dressed to this party. After all, I am the great Mr Stamp-About."

"Yes, sir," said Button, not daring to say any more about the old man. "Well, I'm afraid we haven't a coat or umbrella like the ones you bought this morning, sir."

"You storyteller!" cried Stamp-About, angrily, and pointed to the coat and umbrella that the old man had just sold to Button. "There's a coat like mine, and an umbrella, too. How dare you tell such untruths? I'll take those, and you'll have to take a pound off the price just as you did this morning."

"But sir – do listen, sir," began poor
Button desperately, and then gave a yell
as Stamp-About picked up the umbrella
and chased him round and round the
shop with it, shouting all the time.
Goodness, what a man!

"All right. Take the coat and the
umbrella," yelled Button, from behind
the counter. "Leave the money over
there. Don't you come near me again!"

With a loud snort Stamp-About put the money down, took the coat and umbrella and went stamping out of the shop. Button sank down on a chair and wondered what Mr Tidy would say to him when he knew that he had sold Mr Stamp-About the same coat and umbrella that he had already bought that morning. Would he be very angry?

No, he wasn't! When he heard poor Button's tale, he sat down on a chair and laughed till the tears ran down his cheeks. "Oh, my word!" he chuckled. "To think that you were clever enough to sell the old rascal his things all over again! Well, he wouldn't listen to your explanations, so it's his own fault. You can have half the money yourself, Button. You had to pay half-price to the old man for the things, so you can put half the money back into the till and keep the rest yourself."

"Oh, thank you, sir!" said Button. "That will make up for all the frights he gave me. Thank you very much! Whatever would Mr Stamp-About say if he knew he had paid twice for the same things?"

Well, I can guess! But as nobody will ever tell him, it won't matter. It was a very expensive morning for him, wasn't it?

Jane Goes
Out to Stay

Jane was going to stay with her friend Pam. She felt very grand indeed. She had never been away from home before – but here she was, watching her mother pack a little bag with her nightdress and dressing-gown, her flannel, sponge and toothbrush, and a clean dress.

"Shall I pack Bunny for you?" said Mother.

"Oh, no," said Jane. "I know he sleeps with me every night, Mummy, but I'm too big to take a bunny away with me. Pam would laugh at me."

"No she wouldn't. Pam is a year younger than you are, and I expect she takes a toy to bed with her every single night," said Mother. "Very well, I won't put Bunny in."

Jane thought of all the things she would tell Pam. She wanted to make Pam think she was very grown-up and important. She would say, "Pam, do you know this. Pam, do you know that?" and Pam would listen eagerly.

She arrived at Pam's in time for lunch. Pam hugged her, for she liked Jane very much.

"Do you mind being away from home?" she said. "Will you like staying with me? I've never stayed away even one night without Mummy."

"Ah, but I'm older than you," said Jane, grandly. "I'm in a class higher at school, too. I shan't mind staying away from home a bit!"

They had lunch, and then they went out to play. The dog next door barked and made Pam jump.

"Pooh!" said Jane, scornfully. "Are you afraid of dogs? I've got a dog of my own at home. Can you ride?"

"No, I can't. Can you?" asked Pam.

"Oh, yes. I ride every Saturday, on a big white pony called Sweetie," said Jane.

"I gallop. And once I went so fast that everyone thought my pony was running away. But he wasn't."

"You must be very clever," said Pam. "I wish I could do things like that."

Jane chose all the games, and she chose ones she was quite the best in. She could run faster than Pam, and she could jump higher.

"Mummy, Jane is wonderful," said Pam, when they went in to tea. "She does everything so well. And she's not a bit afraid of dogs or horses – or of tigers, either, are you, Jane?"

"I don't expect I would be, if I met one," said Jane, pleased at all this praise. "I like animals. You ought to like animals, too, Pam, then you wouldn't be so scared when you see a big dog, or hear a cow moo."

After tea they played card games. Jane was much quicker at them than Pam. She snapped everything and won four games straight off. Pam looked a little sad.

"I wish I could win once," she said.

"Have a game of Happy Families. You may win then," said her mother, feeling

rather sorry for the smaller girl. She thought that Jane might just let Pam win once, to please her. But no, Jane won Happy Families, too.

"I'm stupid, aren't I?" said poor Pam, almost in tears. "I wish I was as wonderful as Jane, Mummy. She can do everything. Jane, do you ever cry?"

"Oh, no," said Jane. But this wasn't quite true. She did cry sometimes.

"Not even when you fall down and hurt your knee?" asked Pam.

"Of course not!" said Jane. "I'm not such a baby."

"Are you ever frightened in the night?" said Pam. "Because I am."

"Of course I'm not," said Jane, in a scornful voice. "I just go to sleep, and don't bother about anything, not even thunder."

"You're too good to be true, Jane, dear," said Pam's mother. "And now I think it's bedtime. Hurry up and have a nice hot bath, because it's very cold tonight."

Soon the two little girls were in

separate little beds, eating a nice supper. Then Pam's mother said goodnight to them both and went downstairs.

She came up a little later with Pam's hot-water bottle, and one for Jane, too. But Jane was already fast asleep. So very gently Pam's mother pushed the hot-water bottle, in its soft furry cover, down into the bed beside the sleeping Jane. Jane never had a hot-water bottle at home, and had never even asked for one.

Now about three hours later Jane woke up. She felt a warm patch against her legs. Whatever could it be? She put down her hand and felt it. It was soft and furry and warm. It must be some animal that had crept into bed with her when she was asleep!

"Go away!" said Jane, and kicked out at it. But it didn't move. It just lay against her leg, furry and warm. Jane felt suddenly frightened.

She sat up in bed and yelled. "Help! Help! There's a wild animal in bed with me! It's biting me, it's biting me, help, help!"

Pam woke up with a jump. She
switched on the light and stared at Jane.
"Oh, Pam! There's a horrid wild animal
in bed with me!" cried Jane again. "It'll
bite me to bits! I believe it's nibbling me
now! Oh! OHH!"

"I'll save you, I'll save you!" cried Pam, and she jumped out of bed. She pulled Jane right out of bed, and then threw back the covers. She saw the furry hot-water bottle cover, and bent to pick it up and throw it away, thinking it was some animal.

Then she saw what it was. How she stared! Then she laughed. She had a very merry little laugh that went "Ha-ha-ha-ho-ho-ho, he-he." She rolled on Jane's bed and she laughed till the tears came into her eyes.

"What's the matter, Pam?" asked Jane, offended. But Pam was laughing too much to tell her. Then in came Pam's mother to see what all the noise was about.

"Oh, Mummy, oh Mummy, Jane was so funny!" said Pam. "She screamed and yelled and cried because she said she had a wild animal in her bed that was biting her to bits! And I got out to rescue her from the dreadful animal – and it was only her hot-water bottle!"

Then it was her mother's turn to

laugh. "Well, well, well – to think of our brave and wonderful Jane being scared of a hot-water bottle! I slipped it into your bed, dear, when you were asleep."

Poor Jane. She did feel so very, very silly. To think she had yelled like that over a hot-water bottle. And what a pity she had said it was biting her!

She got back into bed, very red in the face. She threw the hot-water bottle out on the floor.

"Now don't be cross as well as foolish, Jane," said Pam's mother. "It really was very funny, you know, and we couldn't help laughing. And don't you think little Pam was brave, to jump out of bed and come and try to save you from the wild animal you were shouting about?"

"Yes. She was brave," said Jane. "Thank you, Pam. You're braver than I am!"

Then they went to sleep. But you won't be surprised to hear that next day Jane was much nicer to Pam, and even let her win two games at Snap!

Foolish
Mr Wop

Mr Wop had three shillings in his pocket, three nice, bright silver shillings. He was going to Mother Hoo-Ha's to buy a sitting of hen's eggs, so that he might have some baby chicks. He was very pleased and proud.

Mr Wop didn't often have three silver shillings all to himself. He was a poor and ragged little man, rather lazy, and not always very kind to other people. He had got the three shillings for digging over Miss Simkins's garden, and he was delighted.

He soon came to Mother Hoo-Ha's and she gave him the sitting of eggs. There were twelve, all neatly packed into a large flat basket.

"Now you walk carefully with those,"

said Mother Hoo-Ha to Mr Wop. "You don't want to go jumping and frisking about with twelve eggs in a basket."

"I never jump, and I never frisk," snapped Mr Wop. "Don't be silly. Here are the three shillings – and mind, Mother Hoo-Ha, if one of these eggs is addled, you'll have to give me another in its place."

Off he went, carrying the basket very carefully indeed. Soon he met his friend Twiddles, and he showed him the eggs.

"Walk home with me, Twiddles," said Mr Wop. "I'd like to tell you all I'm going to do."

So Twiddles walked beside him, and Mr Wop began to talk.

"You know, Twiddles," he said, "people think I am lazy and good-for-nothing, and that I'll never get rich. Aha! Little do they know! Do you see these eggs? Well, I shall have twelve baby chicks from them, and I shall feed them on my kitchen scraps, so they won't cost me a penny. They will get nice and fat – and then, Twiddles, what shall I do?"

"Sell them," said Twiddles at once.

"Quite right, Twiddles," said Mr Wop. "I shall sell them for five shillings each, because they will be so fat. What are twelve fives, Twiddles?"

"Sixty," said Twiddles, who knew his tables much better than Mr Wop.

"Sixty whole shillings," said Mr Wop, in delight. "Well, I shall buy three brushes and a lot of tins of paint with that money, Twiddles, and I shall go round offering to paint everyone's gates and fences! They will be so pleased."

"They will pay you twenty shillings a time for painting their cottages," said Twiddles, clapping his hands. "My, Wop, you will be rich in no time. What will you do with all the money you get for painting other people's houses?"

"I shall buy a big barrow," said Wop, "and I shall stock it with kettles, tins, pans and brushes, and go round calling 'Buy, buy, buy!' And when I've sold them all I shall have a bag full of gold! What do you think of that, Twiddles?"

"I think you're a marvel!" said Twiddles, jumping about in excitement. "What will you do then?"

"Aha!" said Mr Wop, standing still and thinking hard. "I shall – I shall – build myself a little house, Twiddles, with a nice back garden. It shall have blue curtains at the window, a red carpet on the floor, and plenty of vegetables in the back garden."

Mr Wop walked on again, getting more and more excited. Twiddles was excited too. It was lovely to have a friend who was going to be so rich.

"Will you keep pigs, Wop?" he asked.

"Of course," said Wop.

"And a goat?" asked Twiddles.

"Of course!" said Wop grandly. "And a donkey to take me to market. And I shall have lovely food to eat, Twiddles."

"What will you have?" asked Twiddles, his mouth watering.

"I shall have treacle pudding for breakfast every day, and chocolate cake for tea," said Wop, "and I shall have ice cream each Sunday. Aha! Won't I be grand?"

"Can I come to tea with you some-times?" asked Twiddles.

"Yes, every Saturday," said Wop.

"Ooh!" said Twiddles, rubbing his hands in delight. "What will you give me for tea, Wop?"

"You shall have sardines, and marmalade on toast," answered Wop, at once. "That will be a treat."

"Oh, I should hate that," said Twiddles. "I can't bear sardines, and I'd rather have jam than marmalade."

"I hope you wouldn't be so rude as to say you wouldn't eat what I will so kindly be giving you every Saturday?" said Wop, huffily.

"Well, I can't eat sardines," said Twiddles. "They make me ill. You know they do. It would be very unkind of you to offer them to me."

"How dare you say I should be unkind," said Wop, fiercely. "It's very, very kind of me even to say I'll have you to tea each Saturday. If you say another word I will not ask you to tea with me when I'm rich."

"All right, then! I don't care!" said Twiddles, looking as sulky as Wop. "I don't want to come. You are a good-for-nothing creature, as everyone says, and it's just like you to offer me sardines when you know I can't eat them."

"You horrid, ungrateful fellow!" shouted Wop, dancing round in rage. "Take that!"

He boxed Twiddles hard on the left ear. Twiddles sat down on the road, and then got up in a temper. He rushed at Wop and smacked him on the cheek.

"Oh! Oh! Oh!" wailed Wop, in pain. "Oh, you wicked fellow! When I'm rich I'll have you punished, yes I will! And

I'll spank you myself, like this!"

He struck at Twiddles with the basket of eggs. They all flew out of the basket up in the air, and then fell *crash – smash – splash* on the two fighters. Oh, what a mess!

Twiddles and Wop sat silently wiping

the egg from their faces. They didn't say anything for quite a long time.

"I shall never be a rich man now!" wept Wop, suddenly. "My eggs are broken! All my plans have come to nothing! Look at that!"

"Well, I shall never have sardines on Saturdays now, anyhow," said Twiddles. "Never mind, Wop. Come home with me and wash. Then we'll have bread and dripping and forget all about being rich. It's too much hard work to be rich, anyway!"

Off they went, but Wop was very sad.

"I was so near to being rich!" he sighed. "So very near. I shall never get another chance!"

The Little Boy
Who Peeped

Jimmie heard the children next door playing over the fence. They laughed and shouted, and sounded very jolly indeed.

"Why don't you go and play with them?" asked his mother. "I'm sure they'd like you to join them."

"I don't want to go," said Jimmie.

He did want to go really – but he knew what would happen if he appeared over the fence. The others would howl at him.

"Go away! Peeper! Tell-tale! Go away! Here's Jimmie! Nasty little peeping-Tom!" And all of them would turn their backs and have nothing to do with him at all.

You see, he was a little sneak! He was always peeping and prying, poking his nose into things that he'd no right to.

He peeped through keyholes, he peeped through door-cracks, and he told tales about what he saw.

"I saw Jeanie reading a book when she ought to have been doing her homework," he would say. "I saw Harry hiding an apple in his desk, ready to take bites when our teacher wasn't looking!"

"How do you know!" Jeanie and Harry would say. "Oh, you horrid peeper – you must have peeped through the keyhole! You're a peeper and a tell-tale!"

So they wouldn't let him into their secrets or tell him their plans, or even let him play with them. It was horrid.

And now the children next door had a secret. He knew they had, because they whispered about it at school. The next-door children were Peter, David and Ann and he knew that John, Harry and Joan were in the secret, too. They all met together in the next-door garden.

This morning they were all there. It was Saturday morning, so there was no school. They were having a most exciting meeting, Jimmie was sure. He knew they were going to discuss a secret badge to wear. He wished and wished he could find out about it.

But it was no use peeping over the fence. They would see him. They might even throw rotten apples at him because there were plenty lying on the ground.

He couldn't even go close to the fence and listen because that would be no use. They were having their meeting at the bottom of the garden on the side away from his fence.

Jimmie wandered down the garden, pricking up his rather large ears. Could

he hear anything? Yes – he heard Ann's high voice.

"And *nobody* must know about this. It's a secret. We'll all go to . . ."

"*Shhh!*" said everyone, fiercely. "Don't talk so loudly, Ann!"

Jimmie couldn't bear not knowing the secret. An idea suddenly came into his head. Couldn't he make a little peep-hole in the fence that ran at the bottom of the next-door garden? He could easily climb over into the field at the bottom, slip along the next-door fence till he came near where the children had their meetings – and then he could make a little hole to peep through.

"They'd never guess I was outside the bottom fence, peeping and listening!" he thought. "I should know all their secrets then – and serve them right, too, for keeping me out of them. Goodness, it would be a most exciting thing to do."

He wondered when to make the hole. Not in the daytime in case anyone saw him. At night then, when it was dark. Would there be a moon tonight? No, not much of a one. Perhaps enough for him to see a little by, but not enough for anyone to see him.

"I'll take my sharp knife and see if I can find a knot in the wood to cut out," he thought. "That will make a lovely peep-hole. Nobody will ever guess! I'll take my small torch, too. That will give me light if I want any."

So that night, when his mother thought he was in bed, Jimmie dressed again and slipped out into the garden.

There was a little moon, and he could just see his way down the path to the bottom fence.

He climbed over into the field. He crept quietly along the fence till he came to the place he wanted – the fence opposite the corner of the next-door garden where the children held their meetings.

He had to switch on his torch to find a knot in the wood. He ran it up and down the fence. At last, in a spot about as high as his knee, he found a knot that was coming loose. It was very easy to prise it out with his knife.

Plop! The knot fell to the ground – and there, knee-high, was a little hole to peep through.

"All I've got to do when they hold a meeting is to slip out into the field, come here, kneel down and peep through the hole!" thought Jimmie. "Then I shall know everything they're planning."

He knelt down and put his eye to the hole. Of course, there was nothing to see but the darkness. He was just pretending he could see the children meeting

173

together when he felt a hand on his shoulder.

Jimmie almost jumped out of his skin. Was it his father? If so, he was in trouble. His father didn't like peepers! He hardly dared to move.

"Ha! A little peeper," said a strange voice, rather high and trembly. "But what are you peeping at on a night as dark as this? You must have a wonderful peep-hole if you can see anything tonight."

Jimmie turned round. It wasn't his father. Who was it then? He switched his torch on and looked. He was most astonished.

He saw a bent little man, with startling green eyes, a beard so long that he had wound it three times round his waist, and a very horrid smile indeed.

"Who are you?" stammered Jimmie.

"I'm the Peeper," said the little man. "Surely you've heard of me? You should have, if you're a peeper, too. Haven't you heard of my wonderful peep-hole, the most magical one in the world?"

Jimmie began to think he was in a

dream. "No. I've never heard of you," he said. "I'm going home now."

"No, no," said the little green-eyed fellow, pulling at Jimmie's arm. "Don't go home yet. Come and see my peep-hole. Do! You'll marvel at it. I don't often show it to children, I can tell you – but you're a boy after my own heart, I can see. Always peeping and prying, aren't you? Well, you come along with me – you'll enjoy my peep-hole."

"I don't want to," said Jimmie. "Oh, dear, is this a dream?"

"It might be," said the green-eyed man. "You never know. Come along now – see my peep-hole!"

Jimmie went with him. He had to go really, because the little man pulled him along so firmly. He took him across the field, into a wood, stopped at a big tree, pressed a knob in it, and hey presto, a door opened! In they went and the door shut.

"Ah – that proves it is a dream," said Jimmie. "Trees don't have doors in them."

The little man lit a lamp that swung down in the middle of the tree. "Now to show you my peep-hole," he said. "Ah, you'll marvel at it!"

He went to the round wall of his curious room and pulled aside a little blue curtain. Behind it was a hole that shone with a strange blue light.

"My peep-hole!" said the little man, proudly. "I bought it myself from the Green Wizard, and fitted it here. My, the peeps I've had and the secrets I know! You go and look through my peep-hole!"

Jimmie felt very curious indeed. He went over to the hole that shone so strangely. He put his face to it and looked right into it.

At first he could see nothing but a blue light that shimmered and wavered. Then it cleared a little and a picture began to form. The little man came and stood beside him, trying to see, too.

"Look – there's a picture coming!" he said. "Oh, it's of a little boy I often see in my peep-hole."

Jimmie watched. He saw a picture of a small boy about his own size, creeping into a room. He went to a cupboard, and stood listening. Then he opened the cupboard, put his hand in quickly, and took out three biscuits. He shut the cupboard again and went out of the room.

Jimmie stared in horror. The little boy was himself! He remembered quite well going and taking three biscuits one day when nobody was about.

"Nasty little thing, isn't he?" said the green-eyed man. "He's always doing things like that. I often peep at him through my peep-hole! Aha, he doesn't know I'm watching him, does he? Now here's another picture of him."

This time a picture came of a boy creeping into a classroom and going to somebody's desk. He took out a book. He dropped blobs of ink over two pages, shut the book and put it back. Then he crept out of the room again.

"Look at that!" said the little man. "Talk about being spiteful! You wouldn't believe anyone could do a thing like that, would you?"

Jimmie felt sick. The boy was himself

again. He remembered playing that horrid trick on Harry, when Harry wouldn't tell him a secret. He had spoilt Harry's composition, and poor Harry had been bottom of the form in that.

"I don't want to look any more," he said, and tried to move away from the peep-hole. But the little man stuck his elbow hard into him and he had to stay there.

"Oh, there's plenty more to see!" he said. "Don't go yet. You'll love the next bit."

Poor Jimmie! He had to watch himself doing so many mean things! He saw himself peeping through the keyhole to

179

watch what Jeanie was doing. He saw himself peeping in at the shed window when Robert and Jack and Danny had a meeting there. He saw himself taking Jane's rubber and hiding Leslie's number book. He watched himself creeping out into the garden on a dark night – and prising a hole in the fence next door!

"My word! It was the same nasty little boy then – it was you!" cried the little man. "I might have guessed it. Well, well, well, to think I've got that horrid little boy here, in my own tree. What shall I do with you?"

He dragged Jimmie away from the peep-hole, and pulled the curtain across it. Then he looked at Jimmie and laughed.

"I'm a big peeper. You're a little one," he said. "I'm a big sneak. You're a little one. Let's be friends. Come and live with me, do."

"No," said Jimmie, scared. He began to shake at the knees.

"Why not?" said the little man. "Don't you like me?"

"No," said Jimmie. "I don't. I don't like myself either."

"Rubbish!" said the little man. "If you didn't like yourself you'd do something about it. Fancy living with a self you don't like! You must be very, very stupid."

"I'm not stupid," said Jimmie. "I didn't know till this minute that I didn't like myself. It was seeing those pictures – peeping at myself – that made me dislike myself. I may be a little peeper and a little sneak – but I'm not going to grow into a big one, like you. So there!"

"Hey, now, stop a minute!" said the little man, astonished. But Jimmie didn't. He suddenly gave the little fellow a push,

rushed to where he thought the door was, opened it, leaped down to the ground and ran for his life!

He bumped into a tree and fell down. He lay there, afraid that the little man would catch him. But he had run right past him, laughing and shouting.

"You can't escape me, Jimmie! I've got my peep-hole! I'll be watching every nasty thing you do. I'll be saying, 'Ah, here's the little peeper again, here's the little sneak!' I'll be watching you, Jimmie."

Jimmie lay there, waiting till the voice and footsteps had died away. Then he got up, found the path and ran home. He undressed and got into bed, puzzled, frightened and very much upset.

In the morning he didn't know if it was a dream or not. "The only thing that I can tell by is whether there really is a hole in the fence next door," he thought. "If there is it wasn't a dream. I'll simply have to find out."

So that morning he climbed over the fence at the bottom of his garden and ran into the field and along the next-door fence. He came to where he thought he had made his peep-hole.

"About knee-high it was," he thought. "Oh, my goodness, there it is – and here's the knot of wood I prised out. It fell in the grass. It wasn't a dream!"

He heard voices on the other side of the fence. It was the six children having a secret meeting again. "Shh!" they said. "Don't talk so loudly, Jimmie might hear. He's probably over in his own garden."

He wasn't. He was quite close by, on

the other side of the fence. He could hear every word if he wanted to. He could peep and see exactly what they were doing.

Well, he didn't. He went away quietly. He was cured for ever and ever of peeping, that was certain. He might even be cured of stealing and sneaking. It's dreadful to think of that little green-eyed fellow using his peep-hole to spy, isn't it? It's enough to make anybody careful!

The
Forgetful Girl

There was once a girl called Bessie who was sent to stay in the country after she had been ill.

Bessie was pleased. She missed her mother and father very much at first, but after a while she loved the country so much that she was very happy indeed.

"I do like the cows," she said to the farmer's wife. "I love the way they stand and stare at me and munch-munch-munch all the time!"

"Oh, so it was you who went into the cowfield this morning," said the farmer's wife, rather sharply. "I wondered who had left the gate open. One of the cows wandered away, and it took me an hour to find her. See you shut the gates after you, Bessie. That's one of the first things

to remember when you are in the country."

Bessie liked the little lambs too. She crawled through a hole in the hedge to get to two little lambs playing together. She told the farmer about them.

"You know, they didn't see me crawl through the hole," she said. "I got right up to them and patted one of them."

"Oh, so it was you who made that hole big enough for the lambs to squeeze through," said the farmer crossly. "Do you know that those two lambs crept out of that hole you made and got into the road? They were nearly knocked down by a car! Please don't crawl through gaps in the hedge and make them big enough for my animals to escape."

Bessie liked the fat, grunting pigs too. She told Charlie, the farmer's son, how she had tickled one with a stick.

"Did you leave the sty-gate open?" asked Charlie. "You're so forgetful that I expect it was you. Well, I had to give up my whole lunch-hour chasing the pigs out of the garden. Now just see you shut the gate next time."

But, you know, Bessie was so forgetful that she hardly ever remembered to shut any gates. Horses escaped, the bull got out of the orchard, and the hens ran out of the yard – all because of forgetful Bessie!

One day Bessie saw the farmer's wife planting seeds in her garden, and she wanted to plant some too.

"Couldn't I have my own bit of garden and grow some seeds there?" she asked. "I would dig it and weed it and water it beautifully. I really would."

The farmer's wife said she might. So she gave Bessie a dear little garden tucked away behind the old wall. It had its own bit of grass and its own small white gate. Bessie was very proud of it.

She planted candytuft, Shirley poppies, marigolds, nasturtiums, lettuce, radishes, and mustard and cress. It was very exciting to watch for them all to come up.

"When Mummy comes down to see me I will give her a bunch of flowers to take home, some mustard and cress for tea,

and some lettuces and radishes to take back to Daddy," said Bessie happily.

She weeded her garden well. She watered the little green seedlings that came up. The farmer's wife was very pleased with her – until Bessie left open the gate of the long field and all the sheep escaped on to the road! Then she was very cross and threatened to take Bessie's garden away from her.

Bessie was very upset. "Oh, please, let me have my dear little garden," she wept. "Mummy is coming soon. I do want to give her flowers and salad."

So the farmer's wife forgave her and let her keep her garden. But one day, when Bessie came home from afternoon school and went to look at all her growing things, she got such a dreadful shock!

Not a thing was in her garden! All the flowers were pulled up. The lettuces were gone. The radishes had been pulled up and nibbled. The mustard and cress were both eaten!

Bessie stood and stared – and then she burst into tears. "Oh, oh!" she wept. "My garden is gone. Someone has been here and taken everything – and I did love it all so."

The farmer's wife came running to see what was the matter. When she saw the spoilt garden she was sad. She looked at Bessie.

"What has happened?" she asked.

"I don't know," wept poor Bessie.

"I think I know," said the farmer's wife, pointing to some little footsteps all over the earth of the bed. "Look," she continued, "those are the footsteps of the lambs from the field. Did you leave your gate open?"

Bessie looked at the little white gate that led to her garden. She remembered how she had left it open and had meant to go back and shut it. And she hadn't gone back. So it had been open!

"And those horrid lambs walked in from the field and ate every single thing!" wept Bessie. "Oh, I don't like them a bit, not a bit."

"It's yourself you should dislike," said the farmer's wife. "It was you who caused your garden to be spoilt, Bessie, by leaving your gate open. It is you who were horrid to yourself!"

Bessie knew it was. She went away into a dark corner of the barn and cried till she had no more tears. She couldn't bear to think of her pretty garden all spoilt and eaten because of her own foolish carelessness.

"Now I know what the farmer felt like when I left the gate open and the horses escaped, and I know how the farmer's wife felt when I let the cows out, and how Charlie felt when he lost his lunchhour because I left the pigsty gate open,"

191

thought Bessie. "And I didn't learn any better. But now that I have made my own self miserable, and I know what it feels like, I'll remember. I won't leave my gate open, or anyone else's either!"

So she didn't. And when her mother came down to see her, the farmer's wife told Bessie that she might pick a bunch of flowers from the garden, and take some lettuces and radishes from there too. Mother was very pleased.

"But I would much rather have had them from your own garden, Bessie," she said. "Whatever happened to all the seed you planted?"

And then poor Bessie went red and confessed. But never mind! It will never happen again. I hope it won't happen to you either.